T0328745

"....Truffaut, in a fit of total creativeness, achieves the noblest and the most moving experience of his career."

—*Le Monde*

He is the director and the supporting actor as well as the author of this magnificent screenplay. The story is based on a true account of the capturing in 1798 of the wild child by huntsmen in a forest in southern France and the efforts of a dedicated young doctor to civilize and educate him.

The
Wild Child

by François Truffaut
and Jean Gruault

Translated from the French

by Linda Lewin
and Christine Lémery

WASHINGTON SQUARE PRESS
POCKET BOOKS · NEW YORK

THE WILD CHILD

WASHINGTON SQUARE PRESS edition
published June, 1973

L

Published by
POCKET BOOKS, a division of Simon & Schuster, Inc.,
630 Fifth Avenue, New York, N.Y.

WASHINGTON SQUARE PRESS editions are distributed in the U.S. by Simon & Schuster, Inc., 630 Fifth Avenue, New York, N.Y. 10020 and in Canada by Simon & Schuster of Canada, Ltd., Richmond Hill, Ontario, Canada.

ISBN: 978-1-4767-9853-0

Truffaut Filmography

The 400 Blows
Shoot the Piano Player
Jules and Jim
Soft Skin
Fahrenheit 451
The Bride Wore Black
Stolen Kisses
Mississippi Mermaid
The Wild Child
Bed and Board
Two English Girls
Such a Gorgeous Kid Like Me
Day for Night

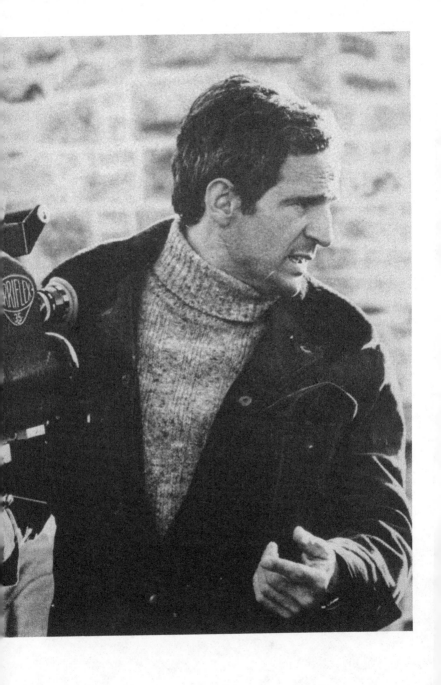

About Truffaut

François Truffaut was born in Paris in 1932. He grew up during the Nazi Occupation of the city and the Second World War. Speaking of his family, he says, "Some of my uncles and cousins were members of the Resistance, and they were deported. Other relatives were collaborators. But my father, who was a draftsman, had only one great passion in life: mountain-climbing. He and my mother would go on frequent mountain-climbing trips and leave me with relatives. I can still remember them returning, wearing shorts and carrying knapsacks on their backs. Our neighbors all looked upon them as eccentrics."

François was a lonely child of a working class family, and he inevitably got into trouble wandering in the streets of Pigalle, the crime-ridden red-light district where he lived.

Like Antoine (hero of *The 400 Blows*), François was always having difficulties in school. When his father was summoned by a juvenile court judge he told him: "Just think, your honor, he hates sports, he prefers to ruin his eyesight in movie houses." The boy forged so many sick notes that the principal called in his mother and told her: "We can't keep your son any longer, madame, his health is too frail." As a teenager Truffaut ran away from home, wandering around Paris and sleeping in subway stations and at the homes of friends whose parents were not around. After two weeks his father found him, grabbed him by the scarf and dragged him to the police station where he was thrown into a jail cell, and from there was sent to a delinquent center. Says Truffaut, "It all happened exactly the way it happened in *The 400 Blows*. But, fortunately, I had met André Bazin, the film critic, before that—when I was trying to start my own *cinemathèque* [film library]—and I was able to write to him from the detention home. He got in touch with the psychologist there and promised that if I were released, he would guarantee me a job."

And so it was that Truffaut later joined the staff of Bazin's *Cahiers du Cinema* where he ultimately became a brilliant, however ruthless, critic. According to Sanche de Gramont (in *The New York Times Magazine,* June 15, 1969), "He laid down the law . . . like a Spanish inquisitor, condemning directors of bad movies to prison and worse, and roasting the 'Oscar collectors' as mere hacks, who, according to commercial requirements, went from a Bible spectacular to a western to a comedy on divorce with no urge to present their own vision of life."

So brutal were his reviews and so innovative were his ideas on the cinema that he was banned from covering the Cannes Festival. Several years later he, along with Godard and other filmmakers, was to be successful in forcing the Festival to shut down to show unity with striking French students and workers.

In 1952 Truffaut, in keeping with his resistance to authority, deserted the Foreign Legion just before his unit was to leave for Indochina. He turned himself in and was released from jail only because of the influence of friends. This incident, along with other autobiographical events, is paralleled in Truffaut's *Stolen Kisses,* where his recurring non-hero, Antoine Doinel, is released from a military prison and is dishonorably discharged.

In 1956 Truffaut began a filmmaking career as assistant to Roberto Rossellini. He kept studying the work of his two idols, Renoir and Hitchcock. After making one short documentary, plus preparing three films that were never produced, in 1958 he made the prize-winning *The Mischief Makers*.

Truffaut's personal life became subordinated to films, and his social life centered around the people of the industry. He was considering marrying either Hitchcock's daughter, Patricia, or one of Renoir's nieces when he met the daughter of a French producer named Morgenstern. With his marriage to her came the $80,000 loan from his new father-in-law, who, exasperated by Truffaut's piercing attacks on the French film establishment, challenged him to go out and make a better film himself. Truffaut did, and the result, *The 400 Blows*, launched his career as one of the world's most celebrated directors. He followed that film with *Shoot the Piano Player* (1960), and after that, Truffaut turned out a major feature about every year. He took time out in 1966 to write *The Cinema of Alfred Hitchcock*.

Truffaut's films reflect many of the experiences of his youth. In particular, he has made four autobiographical films based on the life of his central character, Antoine Doinel, played by Jean-Pierre Léaud, to whom *The Wild Child* is dedicated. Directing the young man in several films, Truffaut became his spiritual father, just as André Bazin had been Truffaut's. *The 400 Blows, Love at Twenty, Stolen Kisses,* and *Bed and Board* tell with great sensitivity of the pains, the joys and the adventures of Antoine growing from childhood through adolescence and into young manhood.

Despite his rebellious youth and unconventional ideas, Truffaut declares, "I am not a revolutionary. . . . The reason that I am not . . . is that I do not trust the next regime any more than I do the one we have now. In temperament, I belong among those people who wish to improve conditions through the existing system, rather than build a whole new system or use a system which may already be known but is highly idealized."

With his affinity for outcast children and youths who reject traditional society, it is not surprising that Truffaut was fascinated with the historical account of the eighteenth-century discovery and capture of a savage child in a forest and the attempts to civilize him. It was the story of those events which gave him the idea of making *The Wild Child,* his ninth film. It won wide acclaim in France and was released to American audiences with great success in 1970.

The story has special relevance for the youth, as well as the educators, of our time. As Robert Geller states (*English Journal,* September 1970), ". . . the child's humanity and pathos are not terribly removed from the increasing numbers of young teens and half-primitives who wander drugged and aimlessly, and sleep in alleys and doorwells throughout America in . . . Market Place, Sunset Boulevard, and Times Square. . . . [The film provides teenagers with meaty material for discussion of] what they themselves have to give up in order to get what they may no longer think is worth getting."

Truffaut's own conclusion is that without society, man is nothing but an animal. Just as Robinson Crusoe was nothing without Friday, man is not really man without his fellow human beings. Without the transfer of a cultural past to his consciousness, man is unable to improve himself or his environment. Those who would gain the most benefit and appreciation from going "back to nature" are those who are highly educated, as was Thoreau.

In this age of contestation and questioning traditional values of western society, Truffaut has presented in *The Wild Child* a probing and very moving cinematic study.

—L. L.

How I Made THE WILD CHILD

by François Truffaut

I have been waiting to make *L'Enfant Sauvage* for three years. One day in 1966, I read an account in *Le Monde* of a thesis by Lucien Malson on "wild children," that is, children deprived of all contact with human beings from their earliest days on, and having, for one reason or another, grown up in isolation.

Lucien Malson described fifty-two authentic cases ranging from the wolf-child of Hesse (1344) to little Yves Cheneau of Saint-Brévin (1968), and among these, the clearest, the most striking and the most instructive seemed to be the case of Victor of Aveyron. When this boy was captured by huntsmen in the depths of the forest in the summer of 1798, Dr. Jean Itard immediately became interested and made the boy the subject of prolonged study.

The "wild child" was covered with hair and moved like an animal, sometimes on all fours, sometimes upright. He was naturally naked, his body covered with scars; his nails were like claws and he spoke only in grunts. He had lived in the forest solely on chestnuts, acorns, and roots, and seemed to have spent seven or eight years there in complete solitude between the time he was abandoned and the day he was captured.

The scars on Victor were the results of fighting, probably with animals he had been struggling with had bitten him, but a deeper one on his neck near the windpipe seemed to have been made by a knife. It is possible that someone had tried to kill the child to be rid of him when he was three or four years old and had

11

left him for dead in the forest. Leaves and dust adhering to the wound may have enabled it to heal by itself. This is one hypothesis, for the mystery of how the wild child of Aveyron was abandoned has never been cleared up.

The boy was taken to the gendarmerie at Rodez and rapidly became an object of public curiosity. The newspapers and gazettes of the day, such as *Le Journal des Débats,* devoted articles to him, and scientists in Paris were soon asking to examine him. He was therefore transferred from the gendarmerie at Rodez to the Deaf and Dumb Institute in Paris, an imposing building in the rue Saint-Jacques which is still standing. The Paris doctors who examined him came to the conclusion that he was a mental defective or idiot child who had been left in the forest for this reason, and was therefore of no interest. They recommended that he should be sent to the Bicêtre hospital for the insane. Jean Itard, a young doctor who was conducting research into deafness, did not share this view. He believed that the wild child of Aveyron was worth educating, and asked to take the boy home with him to his house near Paris and care for him. He undertook Victor's education, using and devising all sorts of methods which are still used today in the re-education of deaf-mutes and backward children.

As a film subject, this fitted the themes that interest me, and now I realize that *L'Enfant Sauvage* is bound up with both *The 400 Blows* and *Fahrenheit 451*. In *The 400 Blows* I showed a child who misses being loved, who grows up without tenderness; in *Fahrenheit 451* it was a man who longs for books, that is, culture. With Victor of Aveyron, what is missing is something more essential—language. These three films are thus built on major frustration. Even in my other films I have tried to describe people who are outside society; they do not reject society, it is society that rejects them.

When I undertook to write the scenario of *L'Enfant Sauvage* with my friend Jean Gruault, the chief difficulty was to transpose the text, which in fact consisted of two reports drawn up by Dr. Jean Itard. The first, dated 1801, was probably meant for the Academy of Medicine; the second, written in 1806, was designed to persuade the Minister of the Interior to renew the pension paid to Madame Guérin, who was caring for the child.

To make a scenario from this material, we imagined that instead of writing his two reports, Dr. Itard had kept a diary. This would enable us to give the story a narrative flow and preserve the author's style with its scientific and philosophical turns, its moralistic and humanistic sides, its homely passages and its lyrical flights.

I therefore remained faithful to Dr. Itard's reports, whose style I greatly admire, and while we were shooting the film I constantly went back to them in order to re-absorb this or that idea or simply to impregnate myself with them again.

I read up on the subject, though not systematically; I simply read a few books on deaf-mutes and Maria Montessori's book. I am always afraid that too much documentation will put me off a subject by making it seem too vast. I like to limit myself from the outset. As it was, I had to limit the length of the film to an hour and a half—and obviously with a subject of this sort, one could pile on details for three hours' showing.

I decided against having a medical adviser during the shooting; I didn't want anybody to stop me from doing certain things. I contented myself with a few consultations, sometimes during the shooting itself. For instance, I was going to use tuning forks, but I didn't want to misuse them. So I asked an ear-nose-and-throat specialist to dinner, and he gave me two or three pieces of precise information on the subject.

With this, I was able to improvise two small scenes on the education of the ear that I should never have been able to think of without this knowledge, but I wanted to avoid anything like systematic technical advice.

Before we started shooting, I had several medical films screened showing autistic children, and I saw that among them there is a great variety of behavior. You have very gentle, very slow children, who do something obsessive—tap on a table all day. You have others who are frantic; you have some who really look like animals and others whose look focuses on nothing. You have still others who live in slow motion. I concluded that I had the right to invent.

The film shows a series of exercises that Itard made the child go through to educate his ear, his eye, and his senses. This is obviously a documentary aspect of the film, and our working criteria were the same as for a documentary: Is it clear, can you understand? An audience had to be able to follow the exercises. At the beginning of each exercise, the audience had to understand what Dr. Itard wanted from the child, so as to be able to follow it from start to finish with interest. This was made possible by using the commentary given by Jean Itard's voice, off-screen, reading his diary.

I now come to the choice of actors. *L'Enfant Sauvage* is a film with two characters. As I saw it, the essential task in this film was not to do the directing, but to attend to the child. I therefore wanted to play the part of Dr. Itard so as to occupy myself with the child personally and avoid using an intermediary. But I didn't make this decision straightaway and, to begin with, the choice of an actor gave me some concern.

First I thought of screen actors, then of television

actors; but I realized it wouldn't do because they would have acted already. There is a certain demand for plausibility in the European cinema, greater than in America. There had been a real Dr. Itard; he had been one of the pioneers of ear-nose-and-throat medicine—not as famous a man as Pasteur, but well-known all the same, and probably better known in America than in France. The film has quite a strong flavor of authenticity, since it is a true story barely "romanticized." Generally, for a film of this kind, one uses actors who are not very well-known. So I went looking for an unknown for the role of the doctor, notably among journalists, then among friends. Finally, since the child never speaks, is practically deaf-and-dumb, and has to be directed within the image, I saw that I should have to try to play the part myself.

I don't know if I was right to do so or not; I don't know if I am a good or a bad actor, but I don't regret my decision. I feel that if I had given Dr. Itard's part to an actor, this would have been the film in which I would have had the least satisfaction, because I should have done a merely technical job in it. I should have been saying to somebody all day, "Now, take the child, make him do this, take him along there," and this is what I wanted to do myself. I am happy that I did it myself. The moment I decided to play Itard, the reason for the film's existence became complete and final for me.

The experience has left me with the impression not of having acted a role, but simply of having directed the film *in front* of the camera and not, as usual, *from behind* it.

For the boy who was to play the main role, I thought of all sorts of children—first of highly educated children, sons of celebrated dancers or children studying dancing at the Opera. Seeing the photographs of Nureyev gave me that idea. I often think Nureyev would

be tremendous in a film where he wasn't playing a
dancer but a wild man.

I set out therefore with the idea of finding a young
Nureyev, then I gave it up because the young dancers
I saw were really too gentle. Then I went in the opposite direction, back to *Les Mistons,* my first film,
where I directed a group of five children from Nîmes,
of whom one had something really very wild about
him. Now, of course, they are married men with
families, because I made *Les Mistons* in 1957. But I
would have liked to find a boy of that sort. I sent my
assistant to watch boys coming out of school at Arles,
Nîmes, Marseille, and so on. In the streets of Mont-
pellier she spotted, among others, a young gypsy boy,
Jean-Pierre Cargol, questioned him and photographed
him. Jean-Pierre, the little gypsy boy whom I finally
chose for the role, is a lovely child, but I think he
really looks as if he had just come out of the woods.

Victor's role might seem a painful one for a child to
play. Directing Jean-Pierre I was constantly trying to
find comparisons. For his expression, I said, "like a
dog"; for the movements of his head, "like a horse." I
mimed Harpo Marx when he had to express amaze-
ment with wide-open eyes. But nervous laughter or sick
laughter were difficult for him to manage, because he
is a very gentle child, very happy and well-balanced,
who could only do tranquil things. Difficult things like
nosebleeds or nervous crises, we only sketched in. We
stopped quite quickly. We avoided the spectacular. The
film doesn't try to frighten or impress people, but to
tell a story.

I know that in this regard making a child play a part
on the screen or on the stage generally has a bad
reputation.

Personally, I don't believe at all that a child's per-
sonality is destroyed by acting. On the contrary. Be-

sides, children are now very well protected by severe regulations governing their work. A committee studies the scenario, doctors examine the child, the headmaster of the school has his say. The "case" goes before a prefectoral commission. The parents may draw only 20 percent of the child's fee, the remainder being paid into his Post Office Savings Account; if the film is made during the school term, a teacher must look after his education, and so on. In the case of *L'Enfant Sauvage,* the chairman of the commission decided to take the film as a test for several reasons: It is a film where the child does nothing shocking, he is not mixed up with stories of gangsters or sex, and he made the film with a team which has the reputation of caring for children very well. I decided to shoot the film in July and August precisely so as not to disturb the child's schooling. Naturally, it is a tiring role; he was therefore given more searching psychological tests than usual. Then, once the film was finished, we saw that the cinema had helped his evolution. In my opinion, the difference between Jean-Pierre Cargol *before* the film and *after* it is astonishing.

The film team presented him with a little 8-millimeter camera at the end of the shooting, and he said, "I'm going to be the first gypsy director."

At the beginning of the film, Victor gets about on all fours; he can't stand upright and cannot bear to wear clothes; he eats like an animal. He begins from nothing, and little by little he adapts himself. As he never became a normal man, a man like other men, it can be argued that it would have been better to leave him in the woods. Like Itard, however, I believe that the life he led there was wretched, and the dozen scars on his body show perfectly well that he had to fight and maybe to kill to survive.

Thanks to Jean Itard, Victor made great progress; he walked normally, he could wear clothes, he was able to perform certain tasks and render simple services, but he never managed to speak, for of all the vital functions, speech is the most deeply linked to early childhood.

It was Jean Itard who chose the name Victor for the wild child, because he noticed that the child was particularly sensitive to the sound "o," and never failed to turn around when he heard somebody say it behind him.

I believe that the strength of this story lies in the situation; this child grew up apart from civilization, so that everything he does in the film he is doing for the first time. When he agrees to lie down on a bed instead of on the ground, it is for the first time; when he puts on clothes, it is for the first time; when he eats at a table, it is for the first time. He sneezes for the first time and sheds his first tears. In my opinion, each step forward means a tremendous piece of luck, and the film draws its strength from all these accumulated steps.

For those who would like to know the end of the real story, which is not shown, Victor lived until he was forty, remaining in the care of Madame Guérin, Jean Itard's housekeeper, in a little house in the rue des Feuillantines which was a dependency of the Deaf and Dumb Institute. He performed simple services and lived quietly.

As to the moral of the story, Malson's study emphasizes it and I think the film brings it out: We inherit what is natural, but culture can come only through education. Hence the importance of this education and the beauty of the subject.

—March, 1970

The
Wild Child

Credits

Scenario: François Truffaut and Jean Gruault
based on *The Memorandum and Report on Victor
de l'Aveyron by Jean Itard* (1806)

Director: François Truffaut

Director of Photography: Nestor Almendros

A co-production of *Les Films du Carrosse* and
United Artists
Distributed by United Artists
The film is available for rental in 16 mm.

The dedication appears:

"TO JEAN-PIERRE LEAUD"

It is followed by this announcement:

"This story is authentic:
it opens in 1798,
in a French forest."

Cast

The Wild Child, Victor of Aveyron	*Jean-Pierre Cargol*
Doctor Jean Itard, Doctor at the Institute for Deaf-Mutes	*François Truffaut*
Madame Guérin, Dr. Itard's housekeeper	*Françoise Seigner*
Rémy, an old peasant	*Paul Ville*
Philippe Pinel, Professor at the Faculty of Medicine	*Jean Daste*
Attendant at the Institute for Deaf-Mutes	*Pierre Fabre*
Monsieur Lémeri	*Claude Miler*
Madame Lémeri	*Annie Miler*

A forest in the district of Aveyron.

Exterior dawn.

Fade up showing a peasant woman squatting and gathering mushrooms at the foot of the trees in the forest. She puts the mushrooms into a wide, shallow basket that she is carrying on her arm. She is in her fifties. She is making her way toward us. Suddenly, against the gentle rustling and the continuous chirping around her, she hears a different sound, as of a cracking branch. She stops walking and, puzzled, turns around in the direction of the noise. She looks up.

Leaves are moving, although there is no wind; abstract shadows produced by the sun's rays suddenly seem to be stirring. The peasant woman listens, then resumes her work, gathering mushrooms and placing them carefully into her basket. She goes to another tree, bends down . . . and suddenly she hears a louder crack of a branch. She stands up again quickly, examining everything around her with a puzzled look on her face.

A few feet away from her she sees several branches near the ground which are moving, and some form of creature—man or beast—becomes noticeable in the dappling sunlight. Under the branches, this "animal," with a strange panting, is scratching the earth and sending it flying into the air.

Although anxious, the woman is still staring at her unusual apparition. Through the flying leaves and dirt, she now perceives the black shape of a curious animal. Frightened, she drops her basket of mushrooms and runs off.

23

We *close up* to the object of her fright: It is a child, about twelve years old: The Wild Child. He is naked, with scars all over his body. His hair is black and very long, his face even blacker with filth than his body. His nostrils are quivering, and seem to enlarge as if he were scenting something. We follow him. In two or three swift leaps, he moves over to the spot where the basket of mushrooms is spilled on the ground.

The wild boy is now on all fours in front of the basket and the mushrooms, which he sniffs suspiciously. Then he stuffs a handful of them into his mouth, half crushing them against his face as he does so. As he eats, his eyes move constantly all around.

We close up slowly toward him as he goes on eating and smearing his face with mushrooms, still squatting. Now

he runs down to the stream. There, flat on his belly on a rock, he stretches his face toward the clear running water and drinks as some animals do. After drinking, he strokes the surface of the water and resumes his running through the branches. Suddenly, he stops, rising to a nearly upright position; his muscles tense, like an animal on the alert. And ceaselessly his eyes shift from right to left and back again. In successive leaps, he reaches the foot of a tree and climbs it, as nimbly and quickly as a monkey. He digs his nails into the bark like claws to help himself up.

Dancing sunlight through the leaves and branches. View of the wild child among the foliage. He watching, scratching his head and body. Leaning back against the trunk of the tree, he rocks himself forward and backward.

Zoom out very slowly, revealing the forest. *Iris out.*

The edge of the forest.

Exterior dawn.

General view of the countryside around the forest. Three peasants in their hunting clothes, with their guns and four dogs, are accompanying the woman who had discovered the unusual animal. The woman is in the lead. All of a sudden they stop. She points to the spot of the encounter. They talk to each other in dialect, practically inaudible.

The three peasants split up in different directions, making their way into the forest. We follow one whose dog has probably scented something, for he is pulling at the leash. The peasant makes signs to the others (off camera), calling out, but indistinguishably.

In the forest, the wild boy is sitting on a big stone, near a stream. He is eating something, but suddenly stops, drops it, alerted and listening. He jerks his head around in all directions, then goes to hide under the leaves. Dogs barking in the distance. The hunters walk in the forest, breaking branches as they go; they catch up with two of the dogs that have been let free. The wild boy slips swiftly through the branches and jumps under a heap of leaves. The dogs, barking even more, bound over the stream. The peasants are conversing in their dialect as they follow them.

The wild child is fleeing through the forest. The two free dogs suddenly spring forward in pursuit.

General view of the forest seen from the edge of the adjacent meadow. We distinguish the wild child, who is running away, chased by the two dogs. The hunters are following behind. One of them is holding the other two dogs on their leashes.

The stream: The wild child hops across it and disappears. A few seconds later, the dogs cross the stream. *Another spot in the forest:* The wild child passes very quickly; so do the dogs. We hear the hunters shouting to the dogs, who rush toward a tree, barking at the top furiously. The wild child is hanging on to one of the highest branches by his two arms, and dangling. The two raging dogs bound and bark at the foot of the tree. The wild child is now hanging from another branch. As he swings in order to catch the next branch, it cracks and immediately breaks.

The wild child has just fallen; he picks himself up and dashes off behind a thicket, where the black dog catches him by the wrist. He shrieks, struggling, and with his free hand tries to force open the jaws of the dog. Both of them roll to the ground. The light-colored dog is barking and prancing around them. The child succeeds in releasing his wrist, but the dog's fangs close tightly again around his hand. The wild child attempts to wring the dog's neck. The light dog is still watching them, barking. By forcing the dog's mouth open with his free hand, the wild child is about to break loose his other hand. A peasant hunter comes running forward; he turns around, showing the two other peasants where the fight is taking place.

The child has just freed his hand; he holds the black dog's jaw upward. Then, ferociously, he bites his adversary's throat. Both the wild child and the dog roll to the ground once more, but the black dog now seems overcome and is moaning. The hunters come running up. The child flees on all fours. We hear the black dog's deathlike moaning, while the light dog barks less loudly. The black dog is stretched on the ground, his throat bloody.

From the edge of the forest, we can see the wild child running away, swiftly and easily, now upright like a monkey, now on all fours. He is followed by the light dog, who is barking away, and the three peasant hunters, one of whom is still holding the other two dogs, who are pulling on their leashes.

The wild child spots a fox burrow. He enters it feet first and disappears. The light dog comes up, sniffs, and prances around it, barking. Another dog joins him, stopping at the hole. Then come the hunters. They carry their loaded guns, ready to shoot. They are discussing in their dialect, drowned out by the barking. A hunter squats down to try to see into the burrow while the others tie the dogs up.

The first hunter goes away to get a punk, then comes back to the burrow and gives it to his friend, who lights it with a tinderbox and uses it to fill the burrow with smoke.

In a little while, the wild child comes into view and emerges from the hole. He tries to slip away on all fours between two hunters, but one of them grabs him. He struggles vigorously. Another peasant holds him back and tries to clothe his naked body with a tunic. The wild child twists in all directions.

The hunters leave the forest, carrying the child wrapped in a garment and tied up.

Dr. Itard's office.

Interior day.

Pan from an anatomical chart of a man's face in profile, which is hanging on the wall, to Dr. Itard pacing in his office while reading the newspaper.

> ITARD: "Canton of Saint-Sernin. A boy of eleven or twelve, entirely naked and to all appearances deaf and dumb, seeking roots and acorns upon which he fed, was seen by three hunters in the woods at Caune and caught as he climbed into a tree to elude them. Taken to a nearby hamlet . . ."

While pacing, Itard has reached his high desk, where he can write standing. He takes a pair of scissors from the shelf, cuts out the article he has just read, and puts it into a file on the desk.

Close up on Itard during the Commentary.

> COMMENTARY (*V. O.*): *If I could bring this child to Paris I would be able, by examining him, to determine at last the degrees of intelligence and the nature of the ideas of an adolescent deprived from childhood on of all instruction, and completely severed from others of his kind.*

A small hut.

Interior day.

The wild child gets up from a pile of hay. He has on a patched gown, too big for him. The sunlight coming through the window seems to have awakened him, and dazed, he goes forward on all fours toward the source of the rays. He tries to stand up straight to see out the window, but he cannot get up. He tries to jump. He falls, brutally pulled back because his ankle is chained. He finally manages to get up and furiously bursts through the pane head first. He has cut his face; it is bleeding. The wild child throws himself back onto the hay, tossing nervously, as a young dog would do. Then he bangs his head against the ground, prances and arches himself, and shudders as though he were having a violent fit.

A small hut.

Exterior day.

A policeman arrives, followed by a peasant. A peasant woman is behind them. It is the woman who found the wild child in the forest. They all speak in their dialect. They enter the hut. Outside the door a young girl appears. She squeals from fright as she sees the wild child rush out of the door and escape at full speed. He is bent over and is nearly on all fours. Very swiftly, he goes through the bars of a gate and disappears into the countryside. Shot of the wild child followed by the policeman and the young girl. The policeman catches him. The young girl stops a few feet away. Peasants are approaching. Dogs are barking.

Outskirts of a farm.

Interior day.

The wild child is coming back on all fours, held by the policeman, the young girl, and the peasants. All the children and the peasants of the next village are rushing toward him out of curiosity. Children sneer and prance around this strange "animal." A peasant woman passes through, leading her flock of sheep. Everybody is yelling. The wild child seems lost and wants to go in another direction, but he is surrounded like an animal tethered at the ankle by the rope which a peasant is holding. Children hit him. An old white-haired peasant drags him to a water barrel. He lifts the cloth cover and shows the wild child the water. The child bends down right away and drinks like an animal, greedily, while the peasant, Rémy, strokes his hair as if to calm him.

Dr. Itard's office.

Interior day.

Itard is standing in front of his writing stand. He is writing with a quill pen. *Voice over* of the text he is writing.

> COMMENTARY (*V. O.*): *All over Paris there is talk of nothing but the child captured in the forest, who has been nicknamed "The Wild Child of Aveyron." Public curiosity is at its height, and my learned colleagues Cuvier and Sicard have obtained authority from the Minister of the Interior, Champagny, to transfer him to Paris. The papers relate that after an attempted escape the young savage has been recaptured and is at present secured in the gendarmerie at Rodez.*

Police station at Rodez.

Interior day.

Near the door, there are two policemen posted. In a corner of the room, there is a caged cell. Behind the bars, we can see the wild child huddled up. He is wearing a ragged old frock. He is still as dirty as before and whimpering.

The Commissioner is sitting behind his desk facing us. He is talking to Old Rémy, whose back is toward us.

> COMMISSIONER: The orders from Paris are explicit. We must leave this week. Here, come with me.

We follow the Commissioner up to the door of the caged cell, which he opens. The wild child is still squatting, huddled up. He is moaning weakly. The Commissioner enters, followed by Rémy.

COMMISSIONER: He can't go like that!

The Commissioner walks back and forth in the cell, looking at the child.

COMMISSIONER: He's filthy! He stinks!

Passing in front of Rémy, the Commissioner steps out to get a sponge from the shelf; then he comes back, grabs a jug of water, pours some on the sponge and goes toward the wild child, who springs up furiously and fights him off violently, striking the Commissioner.

COMMISSIONER (*furious*): Ouch! The dirty pig!

Rémy bounces toward the Commissioner, who has pushed himself away from the wild child, and takes the sponge.

> RÉMY: Let me do it. He's calmer with me. He knows me.

Rémy's hand gently parts the child's hair, which almost covers his face, and he slowly washes his cheeks, forehead, and mouth with the sponge. The child is now docile in front of the old gentle-eyed man.

Iris out.

Road in the Massif Central.
[*A mountain area in central France.*]

Exterior day.

A coach drawn by four horses is approaching an intersection. The coach slows down. The coachman talks to the horseman who is leading one of the first two horses.

> COACHMAN (*quite loudly*): We're fording the river.

The coach stops.

> COACHMAN (*in a loud voice*): Everybody out! We're fording the river.

The door of the coach is opened by a young man who gets out; he is holding the wild child on a leash (the end of the leash is tied to the child's ankle). Behind them are Rémy and another passenger. The wild child leaps forward on all fours. We follow the child past the horses and discover a very narrow humpbacked bridge over the river. The horses lead the coach toward the river, while the passengers walk across the bridge. Suddenly, the wild child, who has escaped, appears on the

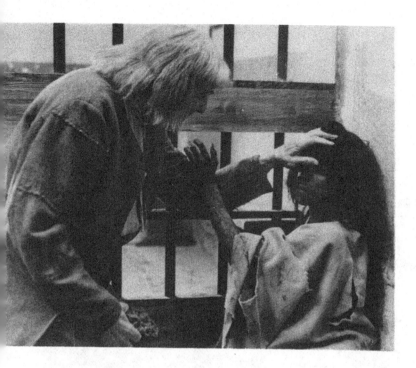

opposite bank and goes to the river to drink, lying flat on his belly. The man who had him on a leash goes to pick him up, and as the child struggles, Rémy intervenes and they all bring him back. Smothered whining.

COACHMAN: Everybody back in the carriage!

Dissolve.

View of the park of The National Institute for Deaf-Mutes.

Interior day.

Dissolve through to the Institute's pool. *Zoom out* to discover the garden of the Institute (the entrance yard) and the buildings. Bells are ringing. *Dissolve.*

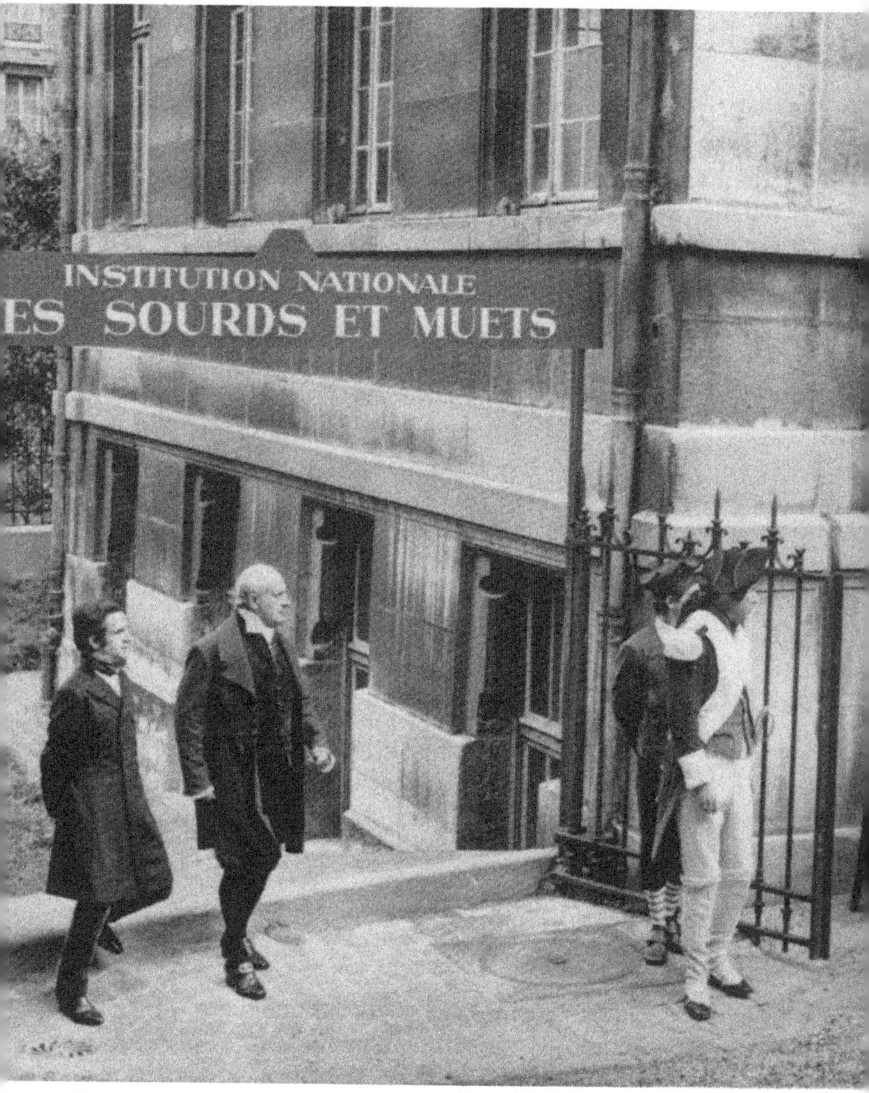
INSTITUTION NATIONALE
ES SOURDS ET MUETS

Dr. Pinel's office.

Interior day.

It is a library-office. Both Doctors Pinel and Itard are standing. Itard is reading out loud an article concerning the wild child. He walks around the room while reading. In contrast to Itard, who is wearing modern clothes and a modern hair style, Professor Pinel, a man in his fifties, his superior in the hierarchy, is wearing a dark, eighteenth-century costume.

> ITARD (*reading while walking*): "To all appearances deaf and dumb, this child seems to use his senses in reverse order: first the sense of smell, then the senses of taste, sight, and finally touch. But he is getting used to human society. The wild child will surely marvel at the wonders of the capital. Hopefully, he will soon be able to tell us the spiciest information about his strange past."

Itard shrugs his shoulders and looks at Pinel.

> PINEL (*amused*): Reread the passage about the wonders of Paris. (*Smiling.*) That's the best!

> ITARD: ". . . human society . . . (*Louder*) . . . The wild child will surely marvel at the wonders of the capital."

> PINEL (*sighing*): ". . . at the wonders of the capital! . . ." No, that's incredible! . . . Really incredible!

Noise of a door being opened. Both doctors turn around.

SECRETARY: Dr. Pinel? Dr. Itard? The wild boy is about to arrive!

On the threshold, the secretary stands aside to let Professors Pinel and Itard pass.

ITARD: Let's go see.

PINEL: Don't be nervous . . . (*Turning around to face Itard.*) Are you happy?

They both leave the room.

National Institute for Deaf-Mutes.

Exterior day.

The gates of the Institute seen from the street. The coach passes. A crowd of curious people runs all around the vehicle. The coach stops; inside we can see Rémy and the wild child in a state of extreme excitement. Itard opens the door of the carriage, and Rémy and the child get out. Itard, with a sympathetic look, wants to help the wild child out, but the child, probably tired out by the long journey and the agitation of the crowd, is looking in all directions.

Itard holds out his hand to the child, who bites it hard.

WOMAN (*shouting*): He bit him! He bit the Doctor!

Pinel looks at Itard's hand.

They lead the wild child away. The gates are shut.

GUARD: Move on. The show is over! The show is over!

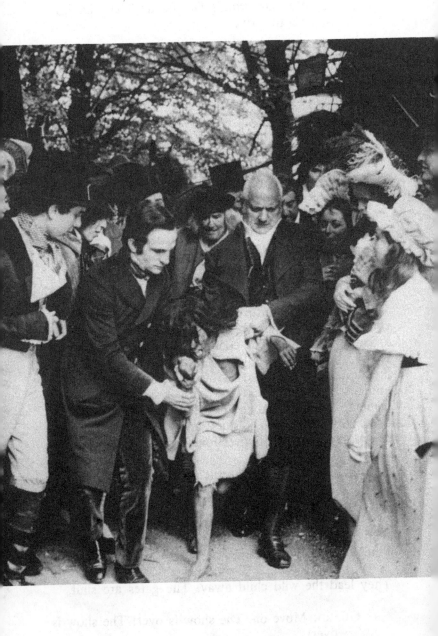

The crowd roars and masses together while Pinel and Itard take the wild child away.

Terrace in the park of the Institute: Itard and Pinel are having problems holding the wild child, who struggles violently. They drag him away toward the buildings. Rémy is following. The deaf-mute children run toward them, squealing with excitement.

> RÉMY (*to the children*): Quiet! Quiet!

They enter the building, followed by Rémy. The camera remains on the doorstep; an attendant seems overwhelmed by the children who want to see the wild child.

Laboratory of the Institute.

Interior day.

Pinel is trying to hold the wild child up straight to measure him. Itard is on the other side; he also helps straighten up the child.

> PINEL (*dictating*): Size: 4.6 feet . . . He must be eleven years old.

Itard raises the yardstick. The wild child sets himself free.

> PINEL: Maybe twelve.

Pinel energetically takes the child's face and examines it.

> PINEL (*still dictating*): Skin, fine, dark. Face, oval. Eyes, black. Long eyelashes. Hair, brown. Chin, rounded. Mouth, medium.

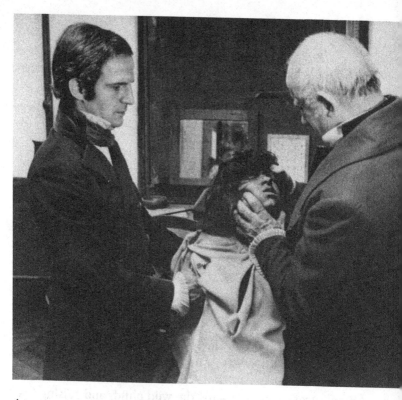

A secretary seated behind a desk writes down everything Dr. Pinel says. Sitting next to the desk is Old Rémy.

    PINEL: Tongue, normal . . .

Pinel holds the wild child's mouth open.

    PINEL (*continuing*): . . . he is not tongue-tied. Dentition, normal. In short, on the surface, nothing distinguishes him from other children.

At this moment, the secretary accidentally knocks something off his desk, a ruler. Everybody turns around except the wild child. Pinel and Itard notice the child's indifference to the noise. Itard looks at the child. The secretary picks up the fallen object. Itard catches Pinel's look.

PINEL: Did you notice? He didn't react. . . . Seat him with his back to the door. I'll try something.

Pinel stands further away. Itard drags the wild child to a chair and sits him down.

Pinel goes to the door, opens it, and slams it hard. The child does not react. He is huddled on a bench, leaning forward as if the changes of his surroundings and his way of life had profoundly affected him. Itard holds him up straight. Pinel joins them again.

PINEL (*positively*): He's deaf.

The three of them go to Rémy, who is sitting.

RÉMY: But in the village, I've seen him turn around when a nut was cracked behind him.

Pinel turns around toward the wild child, and raising his finger, he moves it several times from left to right in front of the child's face . . . without managing to catch his eye. The child is still held up by Itard.

PINEL (*to the secretary*): Write this: "Indifferent to loud noises, whereas he turns around when a nut is cracked behind him. . . ."

The secretary writes. Bells ringing off.

National Institute for Deaf-Mutes: At one of the windows of the Institute, a deaf-mute child is describing the wild child to a friend in sign language, or more precisely, by mimicking the child. We can guess he is describing his hair, his nails, his scars, his teeth, and that his friend, who is also a deaf-mute, understands him perfectly.

Laboratory of the Institute: Itard has his back turned to us in the foreground and Pinel is facing us. Between them is the wild child lying naked on the examination table.

ITARD: Four scars on left arm . . . Scars on shoulder. Two scars on right arm . . . two scars on right leg . . . two scars on left leg.

PINEL (*to the secretary*): About fifteen scars in all.

ITARD (*continuing his examination*): Abrasions . . . lacerations, mostly due to animal bites. (*Pause*) This child surely must have had to kill in order to survive.

PINEL: All these marks on his body tell of battles . . .

The secretary stops writing and looks up. Pinel examines the child's neck.

PINEL: Oh . . . ! There is one which is different from the others. (*To the secretary*) Write this: "When he raises his head, there is visible on the trachea a suture about an inch and a half long. It appears to be the scar of a wound made by a sharp instrument."

The secretary looks up from his notebook again, then resumes writing, nodding his head.

PINEL (*to Itard*): Probably whoever abandoned him meant to kill him?

ITARD: It's possible . . . Yes, I think so, too.

PINEL (*to the secretary, off camera*): Dress him.

Pinel walks forward; he is preoccupied. Itard follows him. They both pass in front of an anatomy chart while talking.

> ITARD: This is how I see it.. For one reason or another, they wanted to get rid of the child by cutting his throat. Probably with a knife. . . . They left him for dead in the forest. And then leaves stuck to the wound and it healed by itself. He must have been three . . . or four. Had he been any younger, he couldn't have fended for himself.

The two doctors are facing each other, still in front of the anatomy chart.

> PINEL: But the wound did not make him dumb . . . and he doesn't speak.

> ITARD: Yes . . . I think the cause of his dumbness is the isolation in which he lived up until now.

> PINEL (*turning*): Look at him.

The wild child is standing, leaning against a large mirror. We see the reflection of the two doctors looking at him; the child is scratching the mirror; he sniffs it, then turns around as if to find the "other" child whose image he sees. Then he moves back and stands puzzled in front of the mirror. Itard (still in reflection) has come up behind him with an apple in his hand. In his impatience to get the apple, the wild child reaches out toward the mirror, scratches it and, not being able to grasp the apple, starts panting. After a while, he realizes that when reaching he gets further from the object he wants, so without turning his head, he reaches back with his hand, a little to one side, and puts it directly on Itard's hand. Itard gives him the fruit. He eats the apple voraciously, watching himself in the mirror. In the reflection Itard joins Pinel.

Itard's home.

Night.

Itard's bedroom, which he also uses as a workroom:
Itard enters his room reflectively with a candle in his
hand (the only lighting in the scene). We follow him up
to his bed; he puts the candle on the bedside table
while he sits on the edge of the bed, facing us. There
is an anatomy chart of a man's profile on the wall.

Attic of the Institute.

Interior day.

A mansard-roofed attic. A deaf-mute child enters and
goes toward the wild child, who is squatting on the
floor wearing the uniform of the Institute. The deaf-

mute child holds out a bowl of soup to him. The wild child scratches his hand in knocking the bowl to the floor violently. The kid runs out and closes the door behind him. The wild child goes to the spilled bowl on all fours. He picks up the scraps of meat that were in the soup and are now scattered on the floor, rolls them mechanically in the dust, and puts them into his mouth after having crushed them against his lips.

Garden of the Institute.

Exterior day.

The young deaf-mutes are playing around the pool, communicating by signs. The attendant passes among them and asks them in sign language where the wild child is. A deaf-mute child points to a manure heap.

ATTENDANT (*nodding*): Oh, yes!

The attendant goes to the dung heap and removes the wild child from it.

ATTENDANT: Oh, there you are! Come along . . .

The attendant lifts up the child roughly and draws him along.

ATTENDANT: Come on . . . You have a visit . . . some high-class visitors!

Since the child struggles, the attendant carries him. The deaf-mute children follow, very excited.

ATTENDANT (*to himself*): I don't know what's the matter with those Parisians. . . . They all want to see you.

Dormitory of the Institute: The attendant takes the wild child into a dormitory and puts him on a bed, while the first visitors come up. These visitors, male and female, carry the latest toys in their arms. They gather around the bed.

ATTENDANT: Here . . . this is the wild boy.

A journalist draws a quick sketch of the child squatting on his bed, ceaselessly swaying back and forth.

FEMALE VISITOR: How old is this child, Sir?

ATTENDANT: Oh, ten or twelve!

MALE VISITOR: Can he talk?

ATTENDANT: No, grunts, only grunts.

ANOTHER MALE VISITOR: Can he hear?

THE ATTENDANT: Well, we don't know. Please, gentlemen, don't put your feet on the bed!

MALE VISITOR: And parents? Does he have any?

THE ATTENDANT: Well, he was found in the woods. So . . .

FEMALE VISITOR: Will he be baptized?

ANOTHER FEMALE VISITOR: What does he eat?

THE ATTENDANT: Mushrooms, roots, acorns.

MALE VISITOR: What about meat? Does he eat meat?

THE ATTENDANT: No, no meat at all, nor anything sweet.

MALE VISITOR: But I heard that he attacked animals.

THE ATTENDANT: Well, that's possible!

ANOTHER MALE VISITOR: He has a normal dentition though.

THE ATTENDANT: Everything is normal.

The wild child bites a too-aggressive male visitor.

MALE VISITOR: Ouch! (*Stepping aside, shocked*) Oh, but he can be dangerous!

THE ATTENDANT: Oh yes, Sir. That happens at times.

SAME VISITOR: You'd better watch him.

THE ATTENDANT: Listen, I'm sorry. All right, ladies and gentlemen, the visit is over.

The attendant pushes everybody toward the door.

FEMALE VISITOR (*disappointed*): Oh . . . ! But listen, it's too short!

THE ATTENDANT: Look, lady, you're not the only one. There's a whole crowd waiting outside.

A MALE VISITOR: The papers exaggerated again.

ANOTHER MALE VISITOR: Had I known he was so stupid, I'd have brought the children.

The visitors go out. The attendant holds the door open, accepting tips from the visitors.

THE ATTENDANT: Thank you, Sir. Thank you, Madam.

The camera stays on the wild child, who is still swaying back and forth in the middle of the toys brought by the visitors; he could not care less about them. The attendant comes back toward the bed and carefully examines one of the toys: a jointed wooden clown.

THE ATTENDANT (*to himself*): H'm . . . not bad!

He takes the toy away with him (we follow him) and swiftly goes to the door. He hides the toy behind a chest of drawers and ushers in a new batch of visitors.

THE ATTENDANT: Please, ladies and gentlemen! This way to see the wild boy.

Men and women come in. The attendant precedes them. A man gives him a tip.

THE ATTENDANT: Thank you . . . This way . . . (*To a pretty woman*) So you've come to see the wild boy?

Dormitory of the Institute.

Interior night.

There are a dozen beds in the dormitory.

Sitting on a chair, a little boy is telling the others a story (*in gestures*). The kids are sitting on the made-up beds watching the story being pantomimed before them.

The attendant comes up and the deaf-mute children rush to their beds.

THE ATTENDANT: It's not finished yet? Hurry and get to bed! . . . Quick!

The attendant then tries to get the wild child to bed. But he fights back, refusing to lie down, and throws his blankets off several times.

THE ATTENDANT (*insisting*): Come on . . . ! Come on . . . ! (*Then discouraged*) Oh well, do it your way!

The attendant goes away. The wild child jumps out of bed, stays crouched down on the floor between two beds, and whines.

Garden of the Institute.

Exterior day.

The children are bullying the wild child near the pool. Itard comes running up, rescues him, and takes him away, pursued by the other children. The attendant intervenes and disperses the children, who are shouting.

Stairway of the Institute.

Interior day.

Itard enters, supporting the child. Pinel meets him.

PINEL: What now?

Pinel seems nervous, but Itard is even more so and replies vehemently to Pinel.

ITARD: This child will end up dying here. The only time they take care of him is when they examine him or exhibit him like a freak.

Pinel climbs up the stairs, followed by Itard still holding up the child.

> PINEL: Listen to me, Citizen Itard, this boy is inferior to all the children we have here. He's lower than an animal.

> ITARD (*sharply*): That's not the point. . . . Or rather, yes: even animals are cared for . . . trained . . .

The two men stop, face to face. The child, very excited, is held by Itard.

> PINEL: You believe he can be trained?

> ITARD: I don't know : . . I don't know . . . But I think there was no point in taking him away from the forest only to lock him up here, as if to punish him for disappointing the curiosity of the Parisians. For, on the whole, that's what they have against him.

> PINEL: Listen . . . if you want my opinion, I think he's an idiot.

Garden of the Institute.

Exterior day.

From Pinel's office window, he and Itard are watching the child in the garden: He is squatting next to the pool, rocking himself back and forth in a pouring rain. He seems happy to feel the rain. From time to time, he raises his face toward the sky the better to enjoy the rain . . . to drink it . . .

> PINEL: I can see no difference between him and the poor idiots I take care of at Bicêtre. You should come with me one day, really.

ITARD: You don't intend to send him to Bicêtre, do you?

PINEL: Well, I see no other way. He can't stay here. It would be better for him and for our deaf-mute children. Don't you agree?

ITARD: I agree that he can't stay here, but I think it would be disastrous to send him to Bicêtre. I don't think he is an idiot. He's just had the misfortune to spend six, seven, maybe eight years in solitude, in absolute isolation.

PINEL: In my opinion, the boy was abandoned and probably stabbed by his parents because he was abnormal. *You* think his isolation made him abnormal.

The child is still swaying back and forth in the rain.

ITARD: Yes.

PINEL: Then why did they abandon him?

ITARD: Probably because he was illegitimate . . . in the way . . . to get rid of him.

PINEL: Do you think you can help him?

ITARD: Yes. I want to try to educate him. This is my wish and I've thought about it since I first read about him in the paper. If the authorities would place him completely under my charge . . .

PINEL (*surprised*): You want to take him with you? To your home?

ITARD: Yes.

PINEL: But how would you manage?

ITARD: My housekeeper, Madame Guérin, will look after him. I live in a house on the outskirts of Paris near the village of Batignolles.

Dr. Itard's house.

Exterior and interior day.

We are inside the house, facing an opened window on the ground floor. Madame Guérin, Dr. Jean Itard's housekeeper, is looking out the window, her back turned to us.

At last, a carriage arrives in the garden. Itard and the child get out and go toward the house. Madame Guérin dashes to meet them. Itard introduces the child to Madame Guérin, who welcomes him in a motherly way.

ITARD: Here's the child.

MADAME GUÉRIN: Hello . . . my boy. You'll be happy here. We'll take care of you.

They take the child along with them to the entrance.

ITARD: You're right, Madame Guérin, he can't understand, but we must talk to him all the same, as often as possible.

In the meantime, they have entered the dining room.

Dining room: Madame Guérin watches the child carefully, and with a gesture shows him the place.

MADAME GUÉRIN: Here's the dining room. Come upstairs. You have to know the house.

They go toward the staircase. The child looks around in all directions.

Staircase: The three of them go up, facing us. Itard helps the child climb the steps; Madame Guérin keeps a close eye on every misstep. It is the first time he climbs a staircase practically by himself, and he has enormous difficulties in doing so.

Itard's office in the house.

Interior day.

Itard is standing in front of his writing stand in his bedroom-office. He is writing in a notebook with a quill pen. We see what he is writing and we hear his voice.

> COMMENTARY (*V. O.*): *I have obtained permission for the child to be entrusted to my care, and my housekeeper, Madame Guérin, will receive one hundred and fifty francs a year from the public funds for her care and trouble. I am aware of the difficulty of our undertaking.*

Itard's house. Kitchen.

Interior day.

We see the child's hands, black with dirt, with long nails—claws—which Madame Guérin is cutting. Then she cuts his toenails while we continue to hear Itard's commentary:

> COMMENTARY (*V. O.*): *What fascinates me with the wild boy is that everything he has done since his arrival in Paris, he is doing for the first time.*

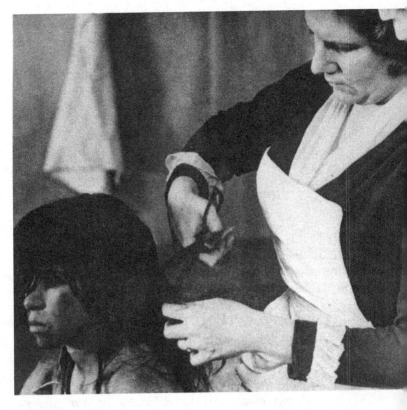

Madame Guérin is cutting the child's hair while he is sitting.

> COMMENTARY (V. O.): *Though he has the habit of sniffing at all he is given, today I have been able to fill his nostrils with snuff without provoking a sneeze.*

The commentary continues while we see Itard trying to straighten the child's shoulderblades so that he will stand up straight.

> COMMENTARY (V. O.): *I must say that for the time being he is insensitive to any kind of moral affection, and that despite the ill treatment he was subjected to at the Institute, he has never been seen crying.*

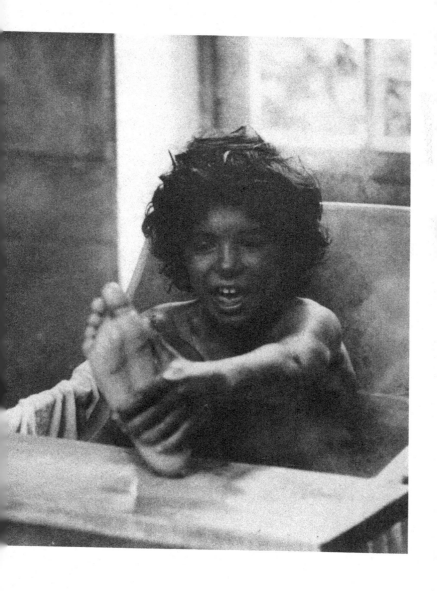

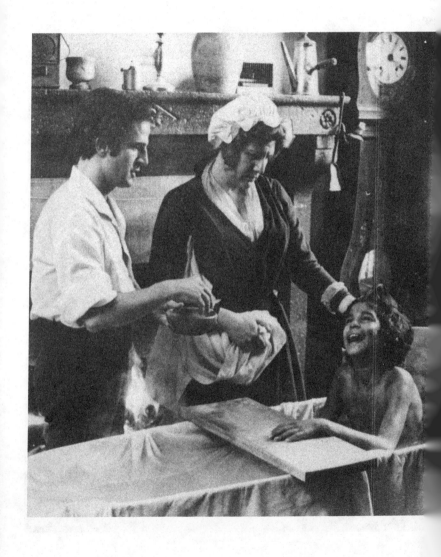

The commentary ends on Itard's hands writing.

Kitchen. Day: The child is sitting in a shoe-shaped bathtub covered with a sheet. Next to him is Madame Guérin, washing him. Itard is busy making a fire in the fireplace. The child is happy. The bathtub is steaming lightly. Itard turns around; he comes toward the tub carrying a pot of hot water.

> MADAME GUÉRIN: Doctor, it's hot enough! I could never stand a bath that hot!

Itard pours the water into the bathtub. The child seems to love it. The heat does not disturb him, though the water is giving off steam.

> ITARD: He can stand it very well. Look at him. You should've seen him in front of the fire when he was picking up glowing embers with his fingers.

> MADAME GUÉRIN: Yes, but aren't you afraid he'll melt like a piece of sugar?

> ITARD: Exactly, I want to soften him up. What he loses in strength, he will gain in nervous sensitivity. (*While Itard is speaking, he fills up a bowl with water, comes back to the child and sprinkles his face with it; the child smiles.*) You have noticed that people from the South are much more open than people from the North. They owe it to the action of the sun on their skin, the heat.

> MADAME GUÉRIN: Doctor, right now I know he doesn't understand us . . . but can he hear us?

The child smiles and shouts gleefully while swishing the water and splashing himself.

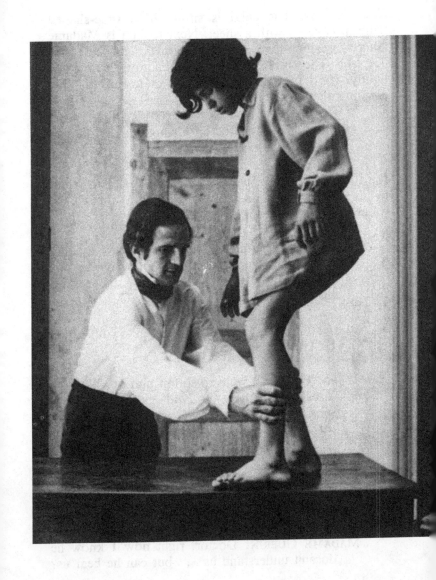

ITARD: He hears us without listening, just as he looks without seeing. We'll teach him how to look and listen.

Itard goes on dashing drops of cold water in the child's face while Madame Guérin is stroking his hair in a motherly fashion.

Itard's bedroom-office: Itard is standing next to the table in the middle of the room. He is trying to teach the child how to walk with straight legs. The child is standing on the table and Itard leads him step by step, holding his calves. He makes him walk two steps forward, two steps backward.

Dining room: Madame Guérin enters, bringing the soup in. She puts it on the table where the child is sitting in front of his plate. He has a napkin around his neck. Itard comes to the table, sits next to the child, unfolds his own napkin and fixes it to his vest. Madame Guérin takes the lid off the steaming soup tureen, while Itard takes a spoon and puts it in the child's hand. Madame Guérin serves the child and passes the tureen to Itard.

MADAME GUÉRIN: Help yourself, Doctor.

ITARD: Thank you.

Madame Guérin sits next to the child, who is playing with the spoon, tapping it against the table. Then he puts his nose into his plate to lap up his soup like an animal.

MADAME GUÉRIN: Oh, God! Give me your hand. . . . There . . . open your mouth. . . . That's better.

She lifts up his head, fixes the spoon correctly in his hand, and makes him eat. The child brusquely grabs the plate, raises it up to his mouth to drink, but spills it on his napkin.

MADAME GUÉRIN: Oh!

Itard hands his own napkin to Madame Guérin, who puts it around the child's neck to replace the one soiled with soup.

ITARD: Here, Madame Guérin . . . We'll attend to that later. He must learn *now*.

Itard refills the child's plate with soup. Without becoming discouraged, Madame Guérin fixes Itard's napkin around the child's neck and begins to feed him again, helping him to use the spoon.

MADAME GUÉRIN: Come on, hold your fingers tight. That's it . . . Open your mouth . . . There . . . Very good.

Slow *iris out* on the child, effecting a *fadeout*.

Child's room. Day: The child wears a pair of heavy cotton pants and a shirt, which he is constantly sniffing. Madame Guérin, who has just dressed him, is sitting facing him.

MADAME GUÉRIN: You see, this is your room. (*Insisting*) *Your own* room, with *your own* bed.

Itard enters the room holding a pair of shoes.

ITARD: Here. This will be his first pair of shoes.

Madame Guérin sits the child down. She begins to put the shoes on his feet while the child rocks himself on the chair ceaselessly.

MADAME GUÉRIN: Help me, Doctor.

ITARD: Yes.

Itard holds the child, who is fighting and whining.

MADAME GUÉRIN: What's he afraid of?

ITARD: He's never worn shoes in his life, you know! He thinks it's to hurt him. Although he must have seen some before.

The child now has the shoes on. Itard steps a few feet away from the child and persuades him to come and join him.

ITARD: Go ahead, take a few steps.

MADAME GUÉRIN (*to the child*): Get up.

ITARD: Lead him to me.

Madame Guérin holds the child and helps him to walk toward Itard.

MADAME GUÉRIN: Walk. Easy . . . there . . . that's right . . .

Helped by Madame Guérin, the child takes a few steps.

ITARD: There, Madame Guérin . . . That's good.

Supported by Madame Guérin, the child walks up to the door where Itard is standing, then back into the room.

ITARD (*to Madame Guérin*): You can let him go now.

The child takes two or three hesitant steps, then falls. Right away, Madame Guérin goes to help him up, but in a mad rage he scratches and tries to bite her.

MADAME GUÉRIN: Ouch! Oh!

The child writhes on the floor in a nervous fit. Itard and Madame Guérin squat near him trying to calm him down.

Itard's office: Itard is writing with a quill pen, standing in front of his writing stand.

> COMMENTARY (*V. O.*): *Little by little, he becomes sensitive to temperature, and we make him appreciate the usefulness of clothes, which he has spurned until now, by leaving him in his room, exposed to the cold in front of the opened window, with his garments next to him . . .*

Child's room. Day: The child is alone, seated on the floor trying to put on his pants; he puts his two feet in the same leg. Behind him, Madame Guérin noiselessly opens the door a crack, peeping into the room, then she closes it.

> COMMENTARY: (*V. O., continued*): *. . . until he decides himself to put them on without assistance.*

For the second time, the door is opened slightly: Madame Guérin and Itard peep into the room and then softly close the door again.

Dining room. Night (it is evening): Madame Guérin is holding a flaming paper. She goes to the child and hands it to him along with a candelabra holding one candle.

> MADAME GUÉRIN: Here, you're going to learn how to light it yourself.

Itard is writing. He looks up to watch the scene. The child lights the candle. The flame reaches his fingers, burning him. He quickly throws the paper down and

thrusts his hand into the opening of his vest. Madame Guérin holds the child's head against her chest.

> MADAME GUÉRIN: Oh, it's nothing . . . it's nothing!

The child sneezes.

> MADAME GUÉRIN (*surprised*): That's the first time I've seen him sneeze.

> ITARD: Yes, I too. Anyway, it's certainly the first time. Look how frightened he is.

As a matter of fact, since his sneezing, the child looks strange; his teeth are even chattering.

> MADAME GUÉRIN (*cuddling him*): Come on, it's time to go to bed, my boy.

Itard resumes writing while Madame Guérin and the child exit.

> MADAME GUÉRIN: Good night, Doctor!

> ITARD (*looking up*): Good night, Madame Guérin.

Child's room. Day: Through the room's window, we can see the child sitting on the floor by the bed, swaying back and forth.

> COMMENTARY (*V. O.*): *Nothing gives greater joy to our little savage than to roam in the countryside. . . . I take him almost daily to a nearby farm, where the kind citizen Lémeri has accustomed him to have milk at tea time. . . .*

Itard enters the room. He is wearing a hat and a cane, and carrying a shirt folded on his arm. The child stands up when he sees him coming.

COMMENTARY (*V. O.*): *I am careful to precede
these excursions by certain preparations which
he may notice: I go into his room about four
o'clock, with my hat on my head, his shirt
folded on my arm, and my cane in my hand.*

Euphoric, the child goes to the closed window and
taps on the pane. Outside, in the garden of the house,
he sees a carriage waiting.

It throws him into joyful excitement; he moves his arms
about, jumping up and down, uttering little sounds.

COMMENTARY (*V. O.*): *It is a curious and moving spectacle . . .*

Country Path.

Exterior day.

The child is joyously sticking his head out of the carriage window. As Itard looks amusedly on, the child
devours the landscape with his eyes. The carriage is
rolling on.

COMMENTARY (*V. O., continued*): *. . . to see the
joy which comes into this child's eyes at the
sight of the hills and woods; the windows of
the carriage barely seem wide enough for his
eager gaze; he leans, now to one side, now to
the other, and shows the liveliest anxiety when
the horses slacken their pace before stopping.*

As a matter of fact, during the commentary the child
disappears sometimes to look out the other side, then
comes back.

As soon as the carriage stops, the child darts out and

rushes into the grass on all fours. Itard gets out also and walks in the path watching the child running ahead, then back to him and around him, and on again. . . . Itard walks on, taking his hat off.

> COMMENTARY (*V. O.*): *The passersby in the countryside would think to see a young lad like other lads, except for his manner of walking which is so singular, indeed heavy since the day he donned shoes, yet ever noticeable by the difficulty he finds in keeping up with my pace and his tendency to break into a trot or a gallop.*

They arrive near the Lémeri house in the middle of the country. M. Lémeri comes out of the house and shakes hands with Itard. The child tries to escape right away, but is held back by Itard. Madame Lémeri, carrying a baby a few months old, comes out on the threshold of the house to greet them. Everybody enters.

The Lémeri house.
Interior day.

Itard and the child enter. Itard greets the lady of the house and gives the baby a slight caress.

ITARD: Hello.

MADAME LÉMERI: Hello. (*Speaking about the child*) I'll give him some milk. (*To the child*) Come.

She goes into the next room with the child and unlocks a cupboard. She takes out a bowl and holds it out to the child. He takes it and holds it out forcefully. She also takes a pitcher out and pours milk into the bowl. As he drinks, the child turns around and looks out the window.

He sees a small boy pushing a wheelbarrow around the garden. He taps his hand against the pane. Madame Lémeri goes up to him.

> MADAME LÉMERI: What are you looking at? Oh, the wheelbarrow. Go . . . go and play with Mathieu, go.

She takes the bowl from him and invites him out into the garden. The child passes through the dining room and goes outside. We stay in the dining room for a moment, just to see Lémeri and Itard sitting face to face with a game of backgammon. They are playing.

The child stops in front of the little boy, who is at first somewhat abashed by the arrival of this intruder.

The two men are sitting facing each other. Itard is not concentrating on the game; he looks toward the garden worriedly.

> LÉMERI: No . . . don't worry! It's all right!

In the meadow, the boy invites the child to sit in the wheelbarrow, then takes the handles and wheels him off.

Both men smile.

The child lets himself be wheeled off, shrieking with joy. The young boy goes faster as he sees his companion's joy.

Itard's house.

Interior day.

In the dining room, the child is setting the table. From time to time, Madame Guérin intervenes.

MADAME GUÉRIN: No . . . the spoon goes here . . . very good!

The child exits to the kitchen; he comes back with the empty soup tureen. He goes to Madame Guérin and pushes it against her for her to take it. Itard is carefully watching the scene through the open window.

MADAME GUÉRIN: What do you want? What are you asking me for?

ITARD (*outside the window*): That's his sign language; he's hungry and is trying to make you understand it.

Itard enters and approaches them.

ITARD: I had already noticed at the Institute that when he was thirsty he'd slap his hand on the jug.

Itard puts his cane and hat in a corner of the room, then turns around and draws the child to him. Madame Guérin steps away toward the kitchen. The child and Itard are in front of the dining table.

ITARD: Come, look!

Handling them like a conjuror, Itard sets three little silver goblets in front of the child. He takes a nut and puts it under the child's nose. The child sniffs it. Then Itard places it under a goblet.

ITARD: Here, I'll show you something.

He mixes up the order of the goblets and then signals the child to look for the nut.

ITARD: You'll look for it by yourself.

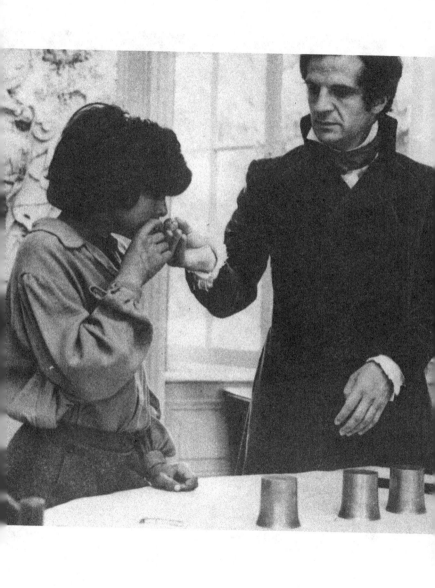

COMMENTARY (*V. O.*): *I strive to capture his attention by various amusements relating to his digestive needs.*

The child's hand hesitates, then moves the very goblet under which Itard has hidden the nut.

ITARD: Very good. Here. (*He takes the nut, breaks it, and puts it into the child's hand.*) Go on, eat it.

The child takes the nut and eats it with pleasure.

The Lémeri garden and house.

Exterior and interior day.

The child crosses the garden followed by Itard. His behavior seems slightly more moderate than before. They enter the Lémeris' dining room through the French doors.

The interior of the Lémeri house: The child goes to the cupboard where the milk is kept. He does not know how to use the key and cannot open it. Frustrated, he strikes the cupboard, then goes to the window and sees in the middle of the meadow the abandoned wheelbarrow without the boy. He comes back to the cupboard and strikes it even harder. Itard, seated and playing backgammon with Lémeri, looks over to see him. He gets up and comes to the child.

ITARD: Wait!

Itard shows him how to turn the key to open the cupboard. The cupboard opens. Itard locks the door immediately.

ITARD (*to the child*): Go on . . . now it's your
turn.

The child clumsily tries to turn the key, but cannot do
it. Itard helps him. The cupboard opens. Itard takes
the bowl, fills it with milk, and gives it to the child.
The latter grabs it eagerly and right away turns around
toward the open window, his back to us. There is a
pause. The wheelbarrow is still there. Suddenly furious,
the child breaks the bowl against the windowsill. Itard
rushes over and chases him.

ITARD: What does that mean? What have you
done? Go on! Go away!

He shakes him and pushes him outside.

The child goes out of the house and walks aimlessly,
turning around several times. He passes near a shrub
in a wooden container, looks at it, and dashes toward
the wheelbarrow. He goes around it, then, determinedly,
goes straight to the house and enters.

The Lémeri dining room: The child goes to the two
men, who are still playing. He takes Lémeri by the
hand and, shouting, pulls him toward him. Lémeri gives
in, gets up, and lets the child drag him out into the
garden.

Garden: The child leads Lémeri up to the wheelbarrow,
striking it to show Lémeri he has to use it. He sits in it.
Lémeri takes the handles of the wheelbarrow and wheels
him around the meadow. The child shrieks with delight.

A path in the countryside.

Exterior day.

Itard is walking on a path. The child cavorts around
him.

COMMENTARY (*V. O.*): *I try little by little to make his excursions less frequent, his meals less copious, his hours abed less long, and his days more profitable to his instruction. By imperceptible degrees I make the game with the goblets more complicated. I am now using objects he cannot eat, for the moment a lead soldier.*

Itard's house.

Interior day.

The child is sitting next to Itard at the dining room table. This time Itard shows the child a lead soldier, puts a goblet over it, and switches the other three goblets. But now the child is paying less attention to the game; his look wanders. Through the open window we can see a big pigeon house. The child is looking toward the window. Itard shakes him out of his daydreaming and, finally, the child makes a mistake, picks up the wrong goblet, then another wrong goblet, then gives up.

> ITARD: Look at the soldier. . . . Find it. . . . It was there. . . . Listen, pay attention to what you're doing.

Itard begins again . . . and the child finds it.

Madame Guérin arrives, her sewing in her hand.

> MADAME GUÉRIN: Bravo!

The child turns around as if he had heard her and leaves the table to go to the window.

Itard watches him curiously.

MADAME GUÉRIN: I think he heard me speak.

ITARD: Yes, it's strange. It's not the first time he's turned around when someone spoke behind him.

Purposely, Itard says loudly:

ITARD: Oh!

The child, his back to us, is looking out the window. He turns around suddenly at the sound of the "oh." He looks in the direction of Itard and taps on the windowsill.

ITARD: I believe he can tell where the sound comes from, especially the sound of "O."

MADAME GUÉRIN: If he isn't really deaf, perhaps he can learn to speak?

ITARD: Perhaps. . . . Remember, it takes an infant eighteen months to learn a few words.

MADAME GUÉRIN: Our poor wild boy! He hasn't even got a name!

ITARD (*getting up*): You're right! But since he is so sensitive to the sound "O," we could give him a name with "O"—Aurelius, Oscar, Nestor . . .

MADAME GUÉRIN: Victor . . .

At "Victor" the child turns abruptly to Madame Guérin.

MADAME GUÉRIN: Did you see that? He likes that name!

She goes over to the child. Itard follows her. Madame
Guérin kisses the child on the forehead.

> ITARD (*looking at the child*): Victor! (*He takes
> him by the shoulders.*) Good! You'll be called
> Victor.

Iris out, stopping two seconds on Victor's face, effecting a *fadeout.*

Dining room. Day: The three are at the table having
lunch. Madame Guérin has her back to us in a three-
quarter shot and Victor is between the two of them. In
the background, the open window.

> COMMENTARY (*V. O.*): *The name of Victor has
> become familiar to him, and when it is spoken
> aloud he rarely fails to turn his head or run
> up; we have agreed, Madame Guérin and I, to
> exercise constantly, without let-up, our pupil's
> attentiveness to the sound of "O."*

Victor is eating almost normally. Suddenly, Itard takes
his glass and, holding it out, abruptly addresses Madame
Guérin.

> ITARD: May I have some *water?* [The French word
> for water is *eau,* pronounced "O."]

He stresses the "O" sound, giving Victor a meaningful
look. Madame Guérin serves him. He drinks.

> ITARD: How cool the *water* is.

Victor looks up from his plate, but he obviously does
not understand what is being demanded of him.

Itard puts his glass down.

> ITARD: I like to drink *water.*

He looks furtively at Victor again. But Victor goes on eating unperturbed. Then Victor holds his glass out to Madame Guérin. Is he going to say "Water?" Itard and Madame Guérin look toward him. Madame Guérin fills the glass, but doesn't give it to Victor, since Itard stops her with a gesture.

> ITARD: No. (*To Victor*) Water! Water . . . water . . . water . . . water . . .

Victor continues to reach out for the glass. He lets out a sort of whistle, but that is all. His body begins to shake. *Reverse shot* of Madame Guérin: She is very distressed to withhold the glass, but as Victor seems to be on the point of a nervous fit, Itard signals Madame Guérin to give him the glass.

> ITARD: Oh, well, give it to him.

Victor drinks greedily, while Itard studies him with concern.

> COMMENTARY (*V. O.*): *What I have not succeeded in obtaining with water I shall perhaps with some other aliment. His liking for milk has already led Victor to express his desire in his own fashion. This happened on the last visit to Citizen Lémeri's.*

The Lémeri house.

Interior day.

Dining room: Madame Guérin is seated. Her husband is standing and comes to meet Itard and Victor, who enter by the French doors. Itard goes and puts down his hat and his cane, while Victor goes toward the table and takes a bowl out of his pocket. He seems to reflect

a second, then goes up to Madame Lémeri and, with the bowl, touches her arm.

> COMMENTARY (*V. O.*): *That day, before our departure from the house, I saw Victor hiding something under his jacket, but I decided not to pay too much attention.* . . .

Madame Lémeri looks at him, then with astonishment at Itard and her husband.

> MADAME LÉMERI: Did you see that?

Itard and Lémeri enter the field of view frame. Lémeri is carrying a backgammon game under his arm.

> ITARD: Well, yes. . . . He broke his bowl the other day, and he thought you wouldn't give him any milk. So he brought his own bowl.

The two men sit down facing each other at the game, while Madame Lémeri gets up and leaves the room with Victor and goes in the direction of the kitchen.

Kitchen: Madame Lémeri pours some milk into the bowl Victor is holding. He drinks while she closes the cupboard.

Itard's house.

Interior day.

Dining room (*seen from the open window*): Victor is facing us, standing up, looking outside, an empty bowl in his hand. In the background Madame Guérin enters the room, holding a pitcher of milk. Itard follows her and stops Madame Guérin.

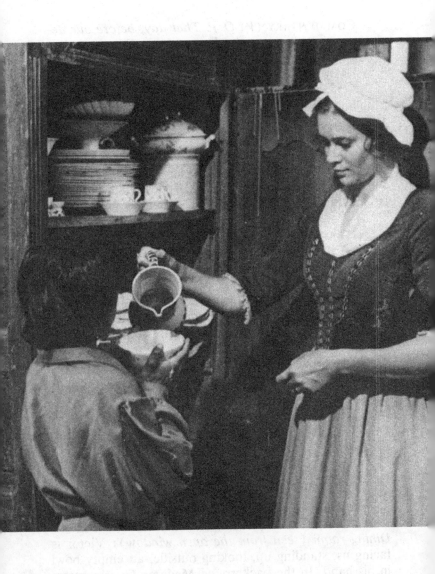

ITARD: Wait, Madame Guérin. You are going to ask me for some milk in front of him.

He takes the pitcher and goes to Victor, whom he gently drags into the middle of the room.

ITARD: Come, Victor . . . come.

All three of them are standing in the center of the room; Madame Guérin is holding a bowl in her hand. Victor has one too. Itard has the pitcher.

MADAME GUÉRIN (*in separate syllables*): I would like some milk . . . *milk*.

Itard pours some milk in Madame Guérin's bowl.

ITARD: Here, Madame Guérin, here is some *milk!*

Madame Guérin drinks. Victor holds out his bowl toward Itard with an appealing look but says nothing. To make himself understood before Itard's inaction, he taps on his bowl.

ITARD: No, Victor . . . no. You must ask for it.

Madame Guérin holds up her bowl. Itard lifts the pitcher to her. Victor turns toward her and taps on his bowl while holding it up to her.

MADAME GUÉRIN *and* ITARD (*at the same time*): No.

Itard then takes a bowl and turns toward Madame Guérin.

ITARD: I'd like some *milk!*

MADAME GUÉRIN (*serving him*): Yes, Doctor.

ITARD: Thank you, Madame Guérin.

Victor, begging more and more, holds his bowl toward Madame Guérin, while Itard drinks.

> MADAME GUÉRIN: Milk . . . milk . . . milk . . . *milk . . . milk . . .*

She caresses his hair.

But Victor still holds up his bowl without saying anything; he even starts shaking nervously.

> ITARD: Give it to him anyway.

Madame Guérin pours him some milk. He starts to drink, but stops, lifts up his head and looks at Madame Guérin fixedly. He seems to be making an effort; he stiffens. And to the great surprise of his two educators, he ineptly lets out the word.

> VICTOR: Mmmilk!

Then he drinks his milk while Madame Guérin and Itard, who are very moved, watch.

> MADAME GUÉRIN: Very good, Victor!

She goes over to Victor, holds him against her maternally, and kisses his hair. He continues drinking, while Itard comes forward facing us and leans on the window-sill.

> COMMENTARY (*V. O.*): *It was the first time that Victor uttered an articulate sound. Madame Guérin heard it with the greatest satisfaction.*

In the background Madame Guérin is seen pouring another bowl of milk for Victor.

> COMMENTARY (*V. O.*): *But for my part, I remarked a fact which greatly reduced the value*

of this achievement in my eyes—it was only at the moment when Madame Guérin, despairing of success, had already poured the milk into his bowl (Itard's hands are shown writing his report) *that the word escaped him.*

Itard continues to write, standing at his writing desk.

COMMENTARY (*V. O., continued*): *I felt that, above all, we should not let it stop at this, and I waited impatiently for Victor to ask for his bowl of milk again.*

Itard's office.

Interior day.

Victor, in the library, finishes drinking a bowl of milk, and asks for another by tapping on the bowl and holding it out in front of him.

ITARD: Victor, ask me for your milk. Milk . . . milk . . .

Itard fills the bowl, but instead of giving it to Victor he holds it back.

ITARD: No, wait. Milk, *milk*. Look what I'm going to do.

Together, they go toward a little corner cupboard. Itard opens it and puts the bowl on a shelf. Right away Victor wants to take the bowl, but Itard pushes it back and closes the cupboard.

ITARD: No . . . no. Victor, no . . . no.

Disconcerted, Victor hesitates for a moment. Itard observes him with curiosity. Victor opens his mouth, but instead of uttering the word "milk," all he does is make a vague grunt. Then he goes resolutely to the cupboard and makes clumsy attempts to open it. Finally, he bangs on the door in a rage and gets on his knees in order to bang better. Itard, somewhat disappointed, goes over, opens the cupboard, takes out the bowl of milk and gives it to Victor, who is still on his knees. He seizes it greedily, but before drinking he lifts his eyes toward Itard and seems to make a great effort.

VICTOR: Mm . . . milk!

Victor, satisfied, greedily drinks his bowl of milk.

Itard watches him with a disappointed look, and goes to the writing desk where he writes in his journal.

> COMMENTARY (*V. O.*): *No, decidedly it is not what I was hoping for. Had Victor uttered the word* before *the thing he desired was conceded, he would have grasped the veritable use of words, a point of communication would have established itself between us, and rapid progress would have followed this initial success. Instead of which, I obtained but an expression of the pleasure he had experienced, insignificant for him and of no use to us.*

Victor's room.

Interior day.

Opening of iris on Victor, dressed, standing in the center of the room with a small mirror in his hand. First he looks at himself, then, catching a sun ray, plays with it, projecting the reflection of the mirror on the walls.

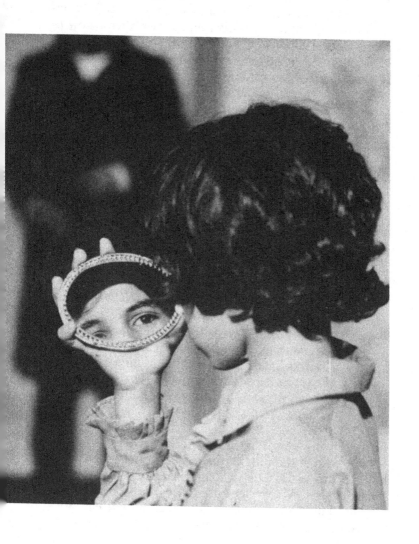

Itard enters, wearing a hat and carrying a cane. He goes up to Victor, who is amusing himself by playing with the sun's reflection and projecting it on Itard's face. Itard waits a little while, seeing the child's delight, then he takes the mirror and shows Victor how to shine the reflections of the sun around the room. He aims at two framed engravings on the wall and then toward the ceiling. Victor is delighted with this. His laughter is less spasmodic.

Iris out.

Itard's office.

Day.

On the table, covered with a white tablecloth, are four tuning forks of different sizes.

> COMMENTARY (*V. O.*): *Victor has been with us but three months and I understand that I was wrong to go too fast. I must first reawaken his hearing; its dullness is understandable.* (Itard's hands go over to the tuning forks.) *In the forest his ears merely served to warn him of the fall of some wild fruit or the approach of a dangerous animal.*

Itard, having taken a tuning fork, advances toward Victor, who is standing in the center of the room. Itard hits the tuning fork he is holding and brings it to Victor's right ear. Victor does not react. Itard turns behind him and hits the tuning fork near Victor's left ear. Victor seems to react and opens his mouth.

Itard and Victor are now seated at a little table. On the table is a mirror facing them (we see a three-quarter view of them, and three-quarters of their faces in reflection). In front of them, placed on two bound books, is a large glass filled with oil with a wick, being used as a candle. Itard is pronouncing some sounds before the flame of the candle.

ITARD: P . . . P . . .

Victor tries in turn but gets nothing but a puff of breath.

ITARD (*insisting*): U . . .

Victor emits a strange whistling.

ITARD: Good! (*He begins again.*) U.

Victor gives a puff of breath without emitting a sound.

ITARD: O.

Victor, surprised, looks at Itard, then takes his turn and tries in vain.

In front of the window of Victor's room: Victor and Itard are face to face and seen in profile. Itard takes Victor's hand and puts it on his (Itard's) throat so that the child can understand the movement of the larynx when Itard emits a sound.

ITARD: A.

Then he puts Victor's hand on his own throat.

VICTOR (*clumsily*): A . . .

The same game with "E," but Victor pronounces the "E" better.

ITARD (*approving with a nod*): That's good.

The same game with "O."

ITARD: O.

Victor tries to pronounce "O." He opens his mouth very wide, but no sound comes out.

Garden of Itard's house.

Exterior day.

Victor is sitting in a chair facing us with his eyes blindfolded. He has a big drum on his knees. In his right hand he holds a drumstick with which he beats the drum. We hear a little bell. At the sound Victor bends down, takes a little bell near his chair, and rings it.

A few yards away, Itard is seated in a chair with the same instruments. Itard taps the frame of his drum with

his drumstick. Victor does the same thing, repeating the sound. Then Itard bangs the skin of his drum. Victor imitates him. Itard knocks on the body of his drum. After a brief hesitation, Victor does the same.

ITARD: Good, Victor!

This time Itard rings his bell and taps on his drum at the same time. Victor laughs with joy and does likewise.

Itard's house. Kitchen.

Interior day.

Victor, seated at the table, is shelling peas. He makes several grimaces while working. Madame Guérin, seated near him, is doing the same work. The noise of the door is heard. Madame Guérin gets up.

MADAME GUÉRIN: Good morning, Doctor.

ITARD: Good morning, Madame Guérin.

Itard enters the kitchen.

MADAME GUÉRIN: He has shelled as many as I have.

She shows the two basins, then she goes toward the sink. In the background, Victor very decidedly gets up and goes to take a key hanging on the wall. Then he goes to another wall near Itard, who is observing him, takes down some small bells hanging on a nail and replaces them with the key. He comes back to the first nail from where he had taken the key and hangs the bells there.

ITARD (*during the child's actions*): Look at him, Madame Guérin . . . look at him.

MADAME GUÉRIN: This morning, while doing the housework, I shifted the objects around. I don't know if you noticed, Doctor, but he has a real passion for order.

Itard caresses Victor's hair.

ITARD: Well, that proves that his memory is functioning and that he can exercise it.

While speaking, Itard leaves the room.

ITARD: I'll be back around noon. I'm going to see the carpenter of Batignolles.

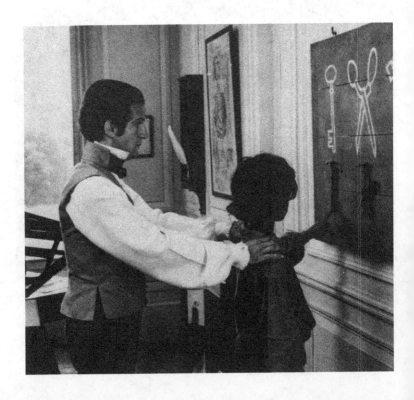

Victor takes a vase of flowers from the buffet, pulls the flowers out, throws them on the floor, and lifts it to drink the water.

MADAME GUÉRIN: Oh! . . . Oh!

Madame Guérin turns to stop him and the boy throws the vase on the ground and breaks it.

MADAME GUÉRIN: Oh!

In dismay, Madame Guérin bends down and picks up the pieces. Victor watches her with astonishment for a moment, then suddenly bends down too, and with a sort of laugh helps her to pick up the pieces.

Itard's office.

Interior day.

There is a blackboard on the wall. Itard's hand draws in chalk a key, a pair of scissors, and a hammer. Then we see Itard and Victor in front of the blackboard. Victor watches him attentively. Then Itard takes a key, a pair of scissors, and a hammer and hangs them on hooks underneath their respective drawings.

ITARD: Victor, look at the key, the scissors, the hammer.

Then Itard unhooks them and puts them in disorder on the mantlepiece. He comes back to the table. Victor starts to follow him.

ITARD: No, wait for me. Stay there.

Itard goes to the blackboard and points to one of the drawings.

ITARD: Victor, bring me the hammer.

Victor remains impassive.

ITARD (*pointing to the key*): Victor, bring me the key.

Victor does not react. Itard points to the scissors.

ITARD: Victor, bring me the scissors.

Victor does not move.

ITARD (*loudly*): Victor!

Itard goes back to the key. Whereupon Victor picks up all three objects on the mantlepiece and brings them to Itard. Itard looks very disappointed as he watches Victor put the objects on the table in disorder.

ITARD: No, Victor, that's not what I wanted.

COMMENTARY (*V. O.*): *I observe that I have probably made a mistake in neglecting to use Victor's natural inclination for order.*

During the commentary, Itard goes to the wall and takes down a chart of the anatomy of the head.

Dissolve.

The blackboard: Under the three drawings are suspended the corresponding objects. Itard comes into view and takes down the objects, then turns to Victor who is out of sight.

ITARD: Victor, hang these things up.

Victor takes the objects that Itard gives him. He positions Victor at the blackboard and moves away. After

CISEAUX PEIGNE L

MARTEAU PLUME CL

a moment, Victor hangs the hammer under the drawing
of the hammer. The same for the scissors. The same
for the key. Then he turns around facing us. Itard
caresses him joyously.

ITARD: Good, Victor . . . that's very good.

Itard takes a glass, fills it with water and gives it to
Victor.

ITARD: There, drink.

Victor, while drinking, walks away. The camera stays
on Itard.

COMMENTARY (*V. O.*): *Victor has always shown
a marked preference for water, and the man-
ner in which he drinks it makes it clear that
he finds great pleasure in it.*

Victor, standing before the open window. He drinks
slowly, while looking at the garden, the trees, nature.

COMMENTARY (*V. O., continued*): *On most occa-
sions, our drinker comes to stand close to the
window, his eyes gazing upon the countryside, as if, in this delectable moment, this child
of nature sought to reunite the two sole bless-
ings which have survived his loss of freedom:
the drink of pure water and the view of the
sunlight and the countryside.*

The garden of Itard's house.
Exterior day.

Victor is sawing some wood. Itard comes over to him
and gently takes the saw away from him and leads him
toward the office.

Itard's office.

Interior day.

Itard is at the blackboard. He rubs out one of the three drawings (the hammer) and draws another in its place.

> COMMENTARY (*V. O.*): *I want to avoid having Victor make each arrangement by memory alone, and I arrive at this by tiring his memory through constantly shifting the drawings around.*

ITARD: Victor! Look at me, Victor!

Victor is not paying attention but looking out of the window.

ITARD: Victor! Look, Victor, look carefully.

While Itard, facing the blackboard, is rubbing out a drawing and replacing it by one he had erased before, Victor slips out of the room on tiptoe. Itard puts down the chalk, turns around and sees he is gone.

ITARD: Victor! Hey, Victor?

He goes and looks out of the window.

Front view of Itard's house.
Exterior day.

Itard appears at a window of the first floor and leans out.

ITARD (*calling*): Victor! Victor!

Madame Guérin is looking out another window.

ITARD: Madame Guérin, have you seen Victor?

MADAME GUÉRIN: No, Doctor. I thought he was with you.

ITARD: Yes, yes, but he's disappeared!

Itard disappears from the window.

MADAME GUÉRIN (*calling*): Victor! Victor!

Itard goes out of the house and walks in the garden, looking right and left.

COMMENTARY (*V. O.*): *For an interminable moment I thought that what I have been dreading since Victor came to live with us had happened—that his fancy for the freedom of the fields, so vivid in him yet, despite his newfound needs and burgeoning affection, had incited him to run away.*

We follow Itard, who approaches a linden tree and turns and looks up.

COMMENTARY (*V. O., continued*): *All of a sudden, a rustle in the linden tree made me look up toward the highest branches.*

Victor is calmly sitting on one of the highest branches, swinging his legs.

ITARD: Victor! What are you doing up there? Come down, Victor . . . come and work.

Victor does not move.

Itard's office.

Interior day.

Victor, his back to us, places the objects above five corresponding drawings; above each drawing the name of the object is written in capitals: SCISSORS, COMB, BOOK, HAMMER, KEY. Victor does the exercise without error. Itard approaches.

ITARD: Very good, Victor! Here's your water.

While the child drinks, Itard erases the drawings, leaving only the names on the board.

> COMMENTARY (*V. O.*): *Encouraged by our first successes, I decided to replace this gross system of comparison by another more difficult. Above the drawing I placed all the letters which form the name of the object represented; then I erased the figure, hoping that Victor will see this procedure merely as a change in the drawing which will continue to represent the object for him.*

Itard pushes Victor in front of the blackboard and gives him the objects.

> ITARD: All right, Victor.

Itard goes out. We see Victor from the back, facing the blackboard. He turns around, disconcerted.

> ITARD: Go ahead! Go ahead!

Itard goes over to Victor again.

> ITARD: Listen, Victor . . . it's like before.

Itard tries hard to make the child understand what is expected of him, but he only makes him feel helpless. Victor lets out a cry, then violently throws the objects down and rolls on the floor in a full nervous fit. Itard bends down to comfort him, but Victor fights, trembles, rages. . . .

Itard gets up and goes out. We continue to see the child roll on the ground, foam at the mouth, tremble. Itard runs to the door and opens it.

> ITARD (*calling*): Madame Guérin! Madame Guérin!

> MADAME GUÉRIN (*V. O.*): What is it?

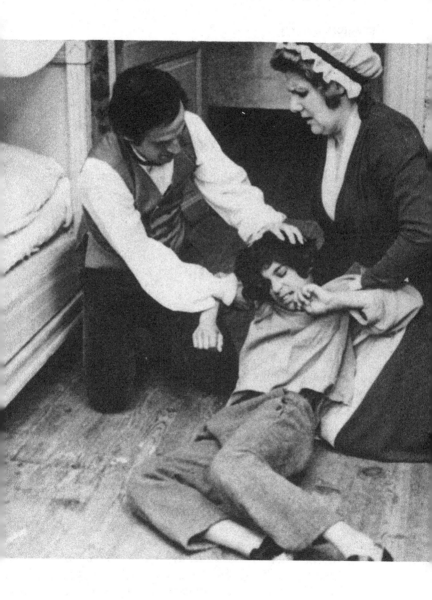

ITARD: It's Victor.

She enters quickly.

ITARD: He's ill, I think.

Madame Guérin crosses the room, shocked.

MADAME GUÉRIN: This . . . this poor child is
exhausted.

She bends down toward Victor, who has calmed down
a little.

MADAME GUÉRIN: Oh! Look, Doctor, his nose is
bleeding.

ITARD: Yes.

Itard bends down.

ITARD: Yes.

Madame Guérin picks him up. Itard helps her. But, annoyed with the doctor, Madame Guérin drags Victor
toward the door by herself while pushing Itard away.

MADAME GUÉRIN: No . . . leave him. This time,
it is I who will take care of him.

Madame Guérin and Victor leave the room. The camera stays on Itard, who closes the door and heads for
his writing desk.

COMMENTARY (*V. O.*): *I have made a great mistake, and if my pupil has not understood me,
the fault is mine rather than his. From the
drawing of an object to its alphabetical repre-
sentation there is an immense distance, and*

the difficulty is insurmountable for Victor at this point in his instruction.

Itard writes with the aid of a quill pen.

> COMMENTARY (*V. O., continued*): *I must therefore seek some method better suited to the still undeveloped faculties of our wild boy, a method whereby each difficulty he masters shall prepare him for the next one he has to overcome.*

A boxed wooden alphabet is shown on the table.

> COMMENTARY (*V. O., continued*): *That is why I had a carpenter from the village of Batignolles make an alphabet in large wooden letters.*

Victor approaches it and places the letters in each corresponding case.

> COMMENTARY (*V. O., continued*): *Victor quickly learned to classify the letters in their correct order, but I have noticed that he succeeds by a ruse, that is, by piling up the letters below the board in their reverse order.*

Itard approaches Victor, who is just finishing putting the letters back into their places in the alphabet box.

> ITARD: That's very good, Victor. After all, you have invented a method which does not need any memory, comparison, and discernment. But I don't mind. This little invention is a tribute to your intelligence.

Itard takes a glass, fills it with water, and offers it to Victor.

> ITARD: Here, drink. (*Victor drinks.*) Now we are really going to work. Let's go.

Itard turns over the box of letters in complete disorder.

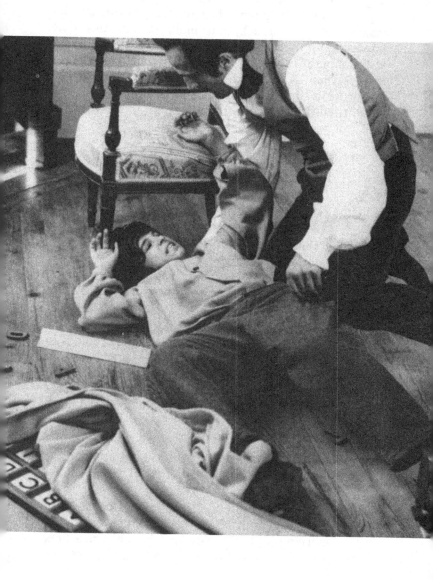

Victor looks at Itard without moving; his eyes have an angry glimmer; he stiffens, then suddenly explodes with rage, throws the alphabet box on the ground, and has another nervous attack, but more serious this time, bordering on epilepsy. Victor rolls on the floor, foams at the mouth, bangs his feet. With difficulty Itard tries to carry him as far as the bed, then puts him to bed. Victor fights and tears the curtains from the canopy. A bit worried, Itard goes to the door and, in the corridor, calls.

> ITARD (*calling*): Madame Guérin! (*She arrives.*)
> It's Victor!

Madame Guérin passes in front of Itard, looking at him severely, and hurries toward the bed, where Victor is writhing nervously. She tries to calm him.

> MADAME GUÉRIN (*very maternally*): Calm down,
> Victor . . . calm down. There, my dear, calm
> yourself.

She takes off his shoes, while Itard, troubled, comes in with a basin of water and a washcloth. Madame Guérin takes the cloth, soaks it in the water, wrings it out by squeezing it very hard, then applies it to Victor's forehead. At each movement, she gives an incensed look at Itard.

> ITARD: His fits of rage worry me. They are increas-
> ingly frequent.

> MADAME GUÉRIN: His fits of rage! Doctor, they
> are your fault! You make him work from
> morning 'til night. You turn his only pleasures
> into exercises—his meals, his outings, every-
> thing!

The child is much calmer; he trembles.

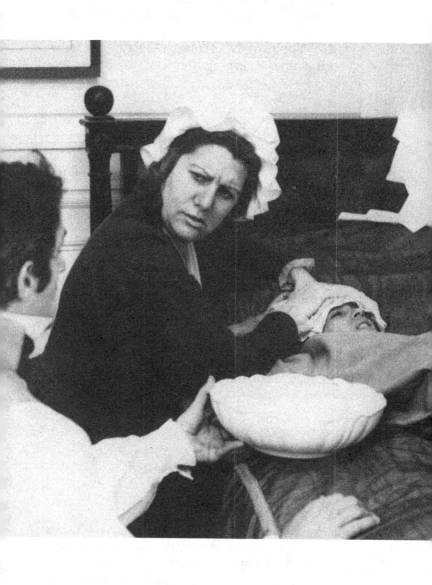

MADAME GUÉRIN (*to Itard*): You want him to catch up in one fell swoop. The poor thing works ten times more than a normal child.

ITARD: You're right, Madame Guérin. I'll make his outings longer.

Country roads.
Day.

Itard, hat on his head and cane in his hand, is walking in the neighborhood. Victor is running ahead of him.

Forest path: Victor turns around Itard, who continues his walk. Victor is very joyous and makes sounds of gaiety. Itard has taken off his hat and is holding it in his hand.

Forest path facing a small hump-backed bridge: Victor and Itard walk toward us. Victor jumps up and down joyfully; he has taken Itard's hat and put it on.

Garden of Itard's house.
Exterior day.

Victor is walking on all fours in the rain. He seems happy and is making joyous sounds. Still on all fours, he gets up on the stoop and looks at the house before lifting his face up into the pouring rain. He is ecstatic.

Iris out on him, effecting a *fadeout*.

Itard's office.

Interior day.

Itard passes in front of the anatomy chart on the wall while buttoning his vest. He goes over to the bed and takes his topcoat and slips it on.

> COMMENTARY (*V. O.*): *Victor has been living with us for seven months and I am not sure of being able to keep him here. Madame Guérin has been in tears since this morning.*

Itard takes his hat and his cane, then, obviously preoccupied, goes out of the room.

> COMMENTARY (*V. O., continued*): *I must go to Paris to plead Victor's cause with His Excellency, for the administration has been persuaded by Citizen Pinel's pessimistic analysis.*

In the corridor Madame Guérin approaches Itard and follows him.

> COMMENTARY (*V. O., continued*): *His observation of certified idiot children at Bicêtre Hospital has led him to establish points in common between those children and the Wild Boy of Aveyron.*

Country road.

Exterior day.

Itard's carriage rolls away down the road.

> COMMENTARY (*V. O., continued*): *These similarities lead to the conclusion that Victor is*

*incapable of being sociable, and that there is
nothing to be hoped from going on with his
instruction any longer.*

Country lane.

Exterior day.

The carriage rolls on.

Itard's house.

Interior night.

While Itard is in Paris, Victor plays with a lighted
candle placed on a table (it is actually a glass of oil
with a wick). Victor turns his head around, looking at
the flame, getting very close, and playing with the flame
with his fingers.

Corridor and Victor's room.

Night.

COMMENTARY (*V. O.*): *His Excellency was unable to receive me; I remain with my anxiety.*

Itard, in the hallway, approaches the door of a room.
He has a candle in his hand and quietly enters Victor's
room. He goes toward Victor's bed. Itard puts the
candle on the night table and sits down on the bed.
Victor sits up right away, takes hold of Itard by the
arms, and pulls him toward him. He takes his hand,
opens it, and presses it to his eyes, his forehead, presses
it to his whole face.

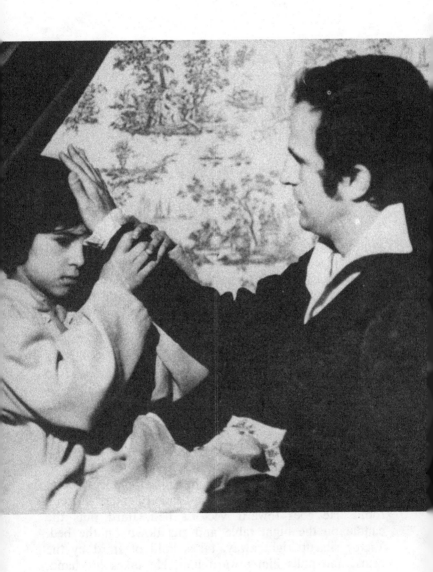

ITARD: Yes, that's your way of talking. But language is also music. Perhaps you will learn it.

Itard's office.

Interior day.

Itard changes the order of certain printed cardboard letters in boxes. He then asks Victor to put wooden letters into the spaces in this new order.

ITARD: Go ahead, Victor, put the letters in their places . . . the new ones, put them in right.

Victor goes up to the table and places the letters in the box.

ITARD: Good. (*Victor places another letter wrong.*) No . . . I don't want the alphabet. (*Victor places another letter.*) Victor, you're mistaken. Victor!

Itard takes Victor's hand and gives him several letters. Victor furiously hurls them to the floor. Itard frowns and points to the letters.

ITARD (*severely*): Go pick them up.

Victor bends down, picks up two letters, goes toward the mantlepiece, bends down and picks up the other letters from the floor. He comes back to the table with the letters and, more violently than the first time, throws them on the floor. Itard furiously rushes toward him, takes him firmly by the shoulders, and pushes him toward a small door.

ITARD: Victor . . . get into the dark closet.

He opens the closet door (it is a small storage cabinet under the stairway) and pushes Victor into it; furious, he bangs against the sides. Itard closes the door. Victor bangs on it. We follow Itard into the room. He goes to the window and crosses his arms.

> COMMENTARY (*V. O.*): *Victor's rages often stop us in the midst of our work. I try to remedy these, not by gentleness, from which one can hope little, but by a disturbing process such as Boerhave used in the Haarlem Hospital. Yet I must not overdo the use of the dark closet, for if this method fails in its effect, I fear that all such treatment will become useless.*

Itard goes back to the closet. He opens the door and lets Victor out. The child has tears in his eyes. Gently, Itard holds his head.

> ITARD: Come, Victor, don't cry anymore. You can do it . . . come.

Itard takes him back to the alphabet box and insists that he put all the letters back into their pigeonholes. Victor does it slowly.

> ITARD: You can do it.

Victor replaces the letters with much hesitation, but docilely, while drying his tears and sniffing. Itard steps away from him, then goes to the table and pours out a glass of water. Victor watches him do it.

> ITARD: Good . . . good, Victor.

Itard shows the glass to Victor.

> ITARD: It's for you, Victor, when you're finished. . . . Good.

Itard goes toward his writing desk. In his journal he makes a note.

> COMMENTARY (*V. O.*): *Today for the first time Victor wept.*

Itard's house. Kitchen.

Interior day.

Coming from the hallway, Victor enters the kitchen and passes in front of the table. Itard is at the table ready for breakfast. Victor sits down opposite him, clasping his empty bowl with both hands as if impatient to drink.

> ITARD: Good morning, Victor. . . .

Victor nods.

> ITARD: Well, look at me.

Itard lays out on the table in front of him the four letters M, I, L, K, forming the word MILK next to his bowl.

> ITARD (*calling*): Madame Guérin!

The door opens. Madame Guérin enters, carrying a pitcher of milk.

> ITARD (*showing the letters*): Look at me. Did I do it right?

> MADAME GUÉRIN: Very good, Doctor.

Itard holds up his bowl. Madame Guérin serves him.

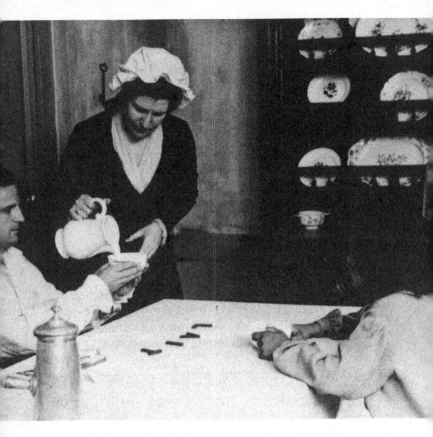

MADAME GUÉRIN: Milk.

ITARD: Milk.

Victor holds out his bowl and taps it with his hand to get some milk.

MADAME GUÉRIN: No, Victor. You know how to write it. Write it.

Madame Guérin puts down her pitcher and walks away, while Victor, who had attentively watched his teacher's stratagem, replaces the letters facing him, simply putting them in reverse order, making "KLIM."

ITARD (*having understood Victor's guile*): Listen, Victor, pay attention.

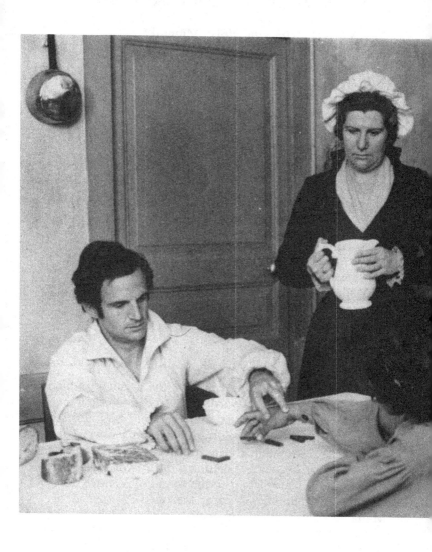

He puts his hand over the letter "M." Immediately Victor grasps the idea and forms the word MILK. At that moment Itard pours the milk into Victor's bowl.

> VICTOR (*with difficulty*) : Mmmilk!

He drinks.

> ITARD: Good.

Itard's house.
Exterior day.

Itard, wearing a hat and carrying a cane, comes out of the house with Victor behind him. They pass in front of Madame Guérin, who is standing at the door. They are going for their customary walk.

> ITARD: We'll see you in a little while, Madame Guérin.

Itard and Victor advance toward the carriage which awaits them in the courtyard. Itard opens the door and starts to help Victor get in. But the child hesitates for a moment, breaks free of Itard, and runs toward the house. He passes quickly in front of Madame Guérin and goes in. Madame Guérin, a little worried, turns toward Itard. Itard listens to the sound of Victor's steps in the house; he stands up at the open carriage door. Madame Guérin looks up at the house and hears the noise of Victor's steps as he leaps down the stairs. He appears, running. He passes in front of her and we follow him up to Itard; he is holding something in his hand that he stuffs into his pocket before meeting Itard, who has him get in immediately. The carriage sets out.

Lémeri house. Dining room.

Interior day.

A round loaf of bread and a basket of vegetables are on the table. Madame Lémeri is sitting near the window, her baby in her arms. Through the windowpane we see Victor arriving in the garden, followed by Itard. Victor approaches and knocks on the pane. Madame Lémeri turns and smiles tenderly. Itard, from a distance, greets her, pushing back his hat. Madame Lémeri gets up, since Victor has just come in. She is about to open the cupboard, but Victor takes her hand and stops her. He looks at her seriously. She turns, surprised; he goes to the table and takes from his pocket several wooden alphabet letters that he puts on the table. He forms the word MILK.

Iris out.

Itard's office.

Interior day.

Victor has his eyes blindfolded; he is seated in a chair facing front.

ITARD (*V. O.*): Pay attention, Victor: "A."

At each vowel Itard pronounces, Victor raises a finger: "A," the thumb; "E," the index finger; "I," the middle finger; "O," the ring finger; and "U," the little finger. Itard's hand closes Victor's each time.

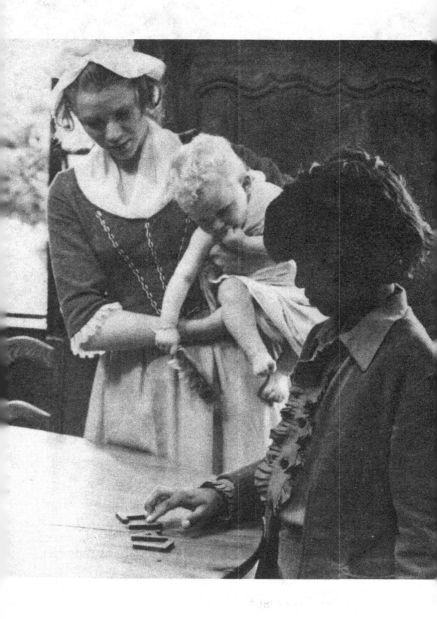

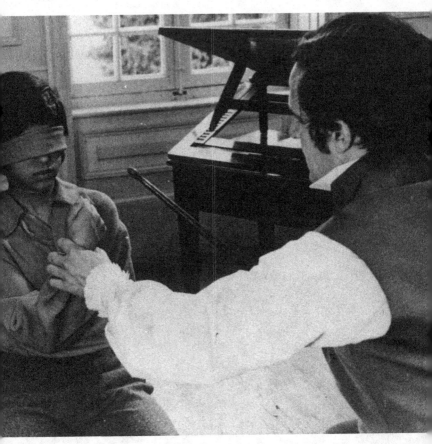

ITARD: Very good, Victor. Very good!

Itard is seated opposite Victor with a ruler in his hand.

ITARD: "I."

Victor raises his thumb and starts to laugh.

ITARD: No, Victor . . . don't laugh, Victor. "I."

Victor raises his index finger and giggles. Itard raps on Victor's hand.

ITARD: Don't laugh, Victor. "O."

Victor raises his middle finger.

ITARD: No, Victor.

He raps. Victor laughs.

ITARD: "U."

Victor, with a big smile, opens his whole hand. Itard raps harder to make the child understand that it isn't a game. The laughter stops at once, and Victor's face clouds over.

ITARD (*very annoyed*): Oh! You're crying! Go ahead, cry! I'm ready to give up.

The camera follows Itard, who passes in front of the blackboard, where the vowels A, E, I, O, U are written, and goes to the window. He turns his back to the window.

ITARD: I'm wasting my time with you. And at times, I'm even sorry we met. I'm discouraged, Victor, discouraged and disappointed!

COMMENTARY (*V. O.*): *Had I not known the extent of my pupil's intelligence so well, I might have thought I had been fully understood, for, hardly had I spoken these words than I perceived, as in his saddest moments, his chest heaving and a stream of tears falling from underneath the gray velvet blindfold. At this moment, as at so many others, ready to renounce the task I had imposed upon myself, how deeply did I regret having known this child, and I condemned the sterile curiosity of the men who first wrenched him away from his innocent and happy life.*

Itard takes Victor's blindfold off. He caresses his eyelids.

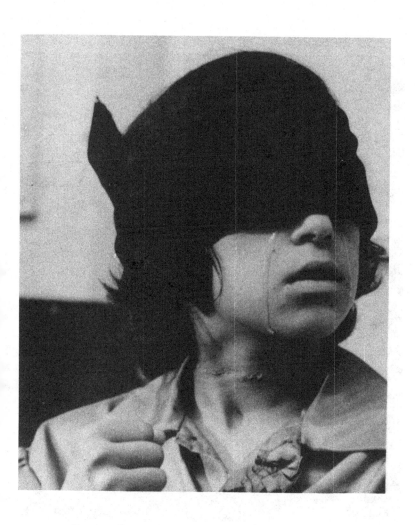

ITARD: Don't cry, Victor.

With eyes closed, Victor remains there motionless. He is still crying.

Black screen.

Itard's house. Victor's room.
Evening.

Itard, carrying a candle, is going to his room. He glances into Victor's room and notices that it is empty. He goes into the moonlit room and walks over to the window.

Through the windowpane he sees Victor in the garden. He is in a prostrate position and seems to be kissing the ground, then he lifts his head and throws kisses to the sky . . . to the moon. Itard, behind the window, also lifts his eyes to the moon. He then lowers his eyes to the garden. Victor is swinging back and forth and walking on all fours in the grass.

Itard's garden.
Exterior day.

A mailman on horseback rides up the roadway leading to the house. Itard approaches him.

MAILMAN: Doctor Itard?

ITARD: Yes.

MAILMAN: A letter for you. (*He gives it to Itard.*)

ITARD: Thank you.

Itard opens the letter while the mailman rides away.

The camera follows him as he walks slowly toward the house, reading.

> COMMENTARY (*V. O.*): *The care you have taken of the child known as the Wild Boy of Aveyron, the changes which have taken place, those which may yet be expected, the interest which so strange a fate and such total abandonment inspire . . .*

Itard passes in front of Victor, who is sawing wood.

> COMMENTARY (*V. O., continued*): *. . . all of this recommends this young man to the attention of men of science and to the protection of the Government. For these reasons, His Excellency has decided to renew the annual pension accorded to Madame Guérin for the care and attention given to your young pupil.*

Itard goes to the door, and, at the threshold, lifts his head.

> ITARD: Madame Guérin! Good news!

He goes in. The camera centers on Victor, who is still sawing wood.

Itard's office.

Interior day.

Victor is at the blackboard, quite clumsily drawing some circles with chalk.

Itard and Victor are shown from the back, each holding a piece of chalk, placing their hands at the same height. Itard draws a straight line. Victor imitates him.

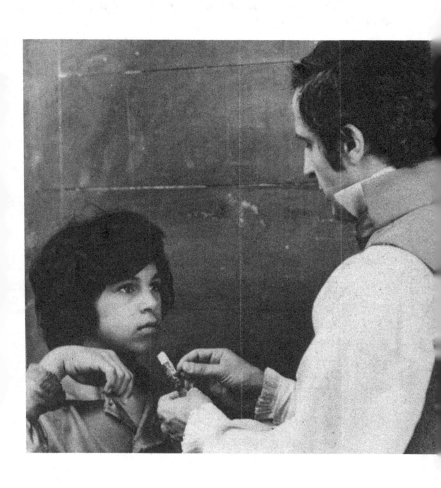

Victor tries to make a circle by himself. He copies from the board the capital letters "A" and "E."

The two are shown from the back in front of the blackboard: Itard takes Victor's hand to show him how to make an "I," then an "A."

The two are facing the blackboard on which is written in big letters the word "VICTOR." Victor is trying to write the same thing under it.

> ITARD (*putting down the chalk*): That's good, Victor. That's *you,* Victor!

Victor shows the written letters, the "R" above and below.

> ITARD: Yes, it's the same. Victor, that's *you,* Victor!

Itard holds the child by the shoulders.

> ITARD: That's *you,* Victor. Do you understand? Do you understand?

> COMMENTARY (*V. O.*): *No, he does not understand, and yet each day brings me fresh proof of his intelligence.*

Victor's room.
Interior day.

Madame Guérin is making Victor's bed. Itard comes in with an object in his hand.

> ITARD: Tell me, Madame Guérin, is it you who made this thing?

MADAME GUÉRIN: My goodness, no, Doctor.

ITARD (*satisfied*): Well, then, it's Victor!

MADAME GUÉRIN: Victor? But . . . that's the old carving knife handle!

ITARD: It's a chalk holder. He made it himself.

MADAME GUÉRIN (*delighted*): How good it is!

ITARD: Ah! . . . Yes, it's very good!

He goes out.

Itard's office.

Interior day.

Itard returns to his office and goes up to the blackboard where Victor is standing. He shows Victor the chalk holder.

> ITARD: Tell me, Victor, is it you who made this? Is it you, Victor?

Victor tries to explain by gestures what he wanted to make.

> ITARD: Yes. It's very good, Victor. It's wonderful. I am very happy.

Itard caresses the child's face for a moment, then walks quickly over to his writing desk. He puts the chalk holder before him and begins to write.

> COMMENTARY (*V. O.*): *Victor has just invented something. Victor is an inventor. One would have had to suffer all the anguish of such difficult teaching, one would have had to follow*

this child in his laborious progress, from the first act of attention to this first spark of imagination, to comprehend the joy I feel, and pardon me for presenting so simple and so ordinary a fact with such ostentation.

Later. Coming from the corridor, Victor enters the office and goes near Itard.

ITARD: Pay attention, Victor!

With a ruler in his hand, Itard is standing in front of a blackboard where the names of different objects are written: "Knife, box, scissors, hammer, comb, bell, key, glass, candlestick, book, brush, picture frame, quill." Each time he names three objects, he points them out on the board.

ITARD: Book. Scissors. Picture frame.

Victor turns around, goes into the corridor, enters a small room where all the objects are displayed on a table. He takes the three asked for and returns, very sure of himself.

ITARD: Brush. Key. Bell.

Victor does the same thing and comes back with the objects.

ITARD: Scissors. Glass. Book.

Same thing from Victor, but a little quicker.

ITARD: Hammer. Comb. Picture frame.

Same thing from Victor, even more quickly.

ITARD: Book. Brush. Candlestick.

Itard looks at the objects Victor has brought.

>ITARD: Bell. Key. Book. Comb. Key. Bell.

Victor runs back and forth between the two rooms with the objects asked for.

>ITARD: Bell. Candlestick. Glass.

Victor hurries in with the three objects.

>ITARD: Key. Brush. Comb.

The objects, then Itard looking at them.

>ITARD: Comb. Key. Bell. Box. Hammer. Glass.

Victor brings the objects very quickly.

Victor is now near the table. The exercise is finished. Itard gives him a glass of water.

>ITARD: Here, Victor, drink. . . . Very good, Victor! That's very good!

Victor drinks near the window.

>COMMENTARY (*V. O.*): *When Victor succeeds in something I reward him, and when he fails, I punish him. Yet I have no certain proof that I have inspired a sense of justice in him.*

Itard is walking in his office.

>COMMENTARY (*V. O., continued*): *He obeys me and corrects himself out of fear or hope of reward, and not from a disinterested awareness of the moral order.*

Itard goes to his writing stand. Victor is in the background drinking by the window.

COMMENTARY (*V. O., continued*): *To throw light on this and obtain a less ambiguous result, I shall be obliged to do an abominable thing. I am going to put Victor's feelings to the test of a flagrant piece of injustice by punishing him without reason, just after he has successfully completed an exercise before my eyes. By putting him forcibly into the dark closet, I shall administer a punishment as odious as it is unjust in order to see, precisely, if he will rebel.*

Itard, after reflecting for a moment, leaves his writing stand and goes to the table on which there are several objects, together with some cards from a game. He sorts the cards for a brief while, then turns around toward Victor.

ITARD: Victor! (*He comes.*) Book. Key. Go on, go . . .

Victor quickly exits. We stay on Itard, who is impassive. Victor comes back carrying the desired objects. He turns to Itard with a smile, convinced that he deserves a just reward for his work. Itard takes the objects, throws them down, and shakes the child by his shoulders.

ITARD: What's this? What do you want? (*He shakes him hard, while Victor struggles, growling.*) What's this? Into the closet!

Itard takes Victor by the arm and forces him toward the dark closet, pulling the door open violently. Victor's usual obedience vanishes; he braces himself against the sides of the door with hands and feet and puts up a stiff resistance.

ITARD: Go in, Victor, go in . . . go!

Itard persists, and tries to lift him to drag him over to

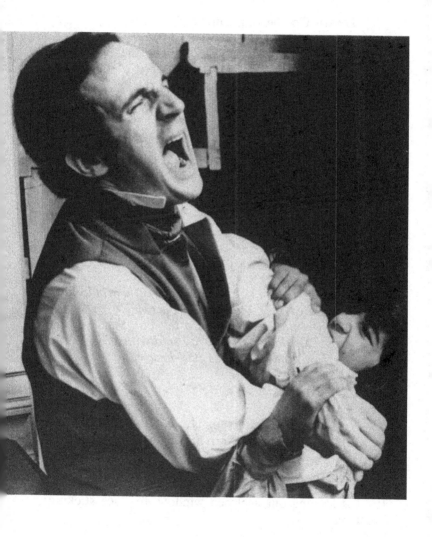

the closet. Victor, indignant and red with anger, struggles in Itard's arms with a fury that almost defeats Itard's efforts.

ITARD: Go ahead, get in!

At last, "feeling ready to yield under the law of the stronger," Victor uses the last resource of the weak: He lunges at his tormentor's arm and bites it.

ITARD: Ouch!

Itard lets go at once. He closes the closet door again and affectionately clasps Victor in his arms. Deeply moved, he says to the child:

ITARD: Victor, that's good, you're right. . . . You were right to rebel. . . .

Itard strokes the child's hair for a long while.

COMMENTARY (V. O.): *How sweet it would have been at this moment to be able to make my pupil understand me, to tell him that the very pain of his bite filled my soul with satisfaction. How could I rejoice half-heartedly?*

Itard's house.

Exterior day.

Itard is looking out a closed window, his face sticking to the pane.

COMMENTARY (V. O.): *I had irrefutable evidence that the feeling of what is just and unjust was no longer alien to Victor's heart. By giving him this feeling, or rather by provoking it, I had just elevated the savage man to the full stature of a moral being by the most drastic of his characteristics and the most noble of his attributes.*

Black fade.

Itard's office.

Interior day.

COMMENTARY (*V. O.*): *Victor has been deprived of his daily outings for a few days, for I am abed with rheumatism. Madame Guérin has called in Dr. Gruault, having forgotten that Victor dislikes nothing so much as the presence of a visitor in the house.*

The door opens noiselessly. Victor peeks in, leans forward, and looks toward the bed where Itard is lying. On the chair next to him is seated the doctor, who is feeling his pulse.

ITARD: Well, Doctor?

DR. GRUAULT: Your pulse is normal. It's a bad chill. I think if you stay in bed a few days, you should feel better soon.

Victor exits into the hallway, then comes back carrying the doctor's hat, gloves, and cane.

ITARD (*to the doctor*): Very well. Thank you, Doctor. I hope that . . . (*He stops, surprised.*)

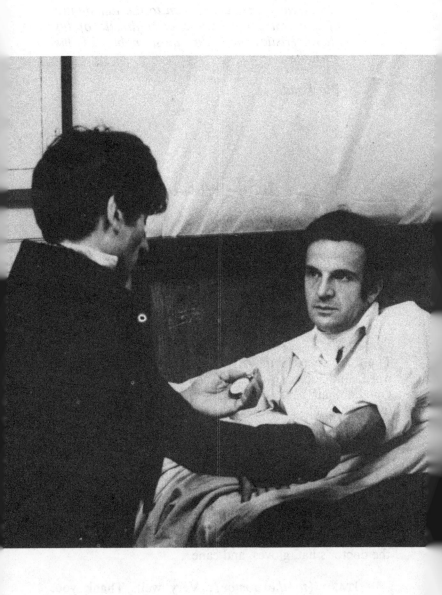

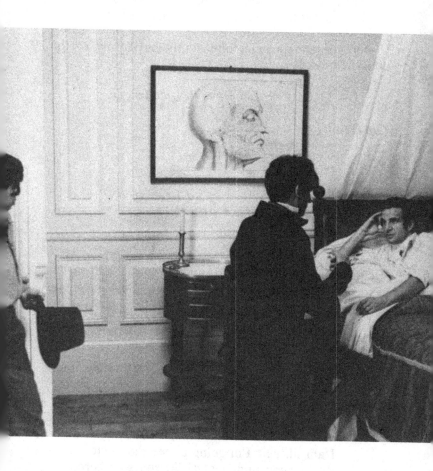

With an unfriendly look, Victor puts the hat on the doctor's head and then hands him his gloves and cane. The doctor takes them with surprise. Then Victor forces him to get up.

ITARD (*shocked*): Hey, Victor!

Victor pulls the doctor by his coat toward the door.

ITARD: Now, Victor!

DR. GRUAULT: Well, I guess . . . our young friend
is putting an end to our consultation.

Victor goes on pushing him gently but firmly to the
door.

DR. GRUAULT: Goodbye, dear colleague.

Lap dissolve.

Itard's house.
Interior day.

Victor comes out of a room, joyous, Itard's hat on his
head. He turns around, making little sounds of delight
as he does when he goes out for a walk.

ITARD: Victor! Victor! I cannot take you.

Itard comes out of his room, squeezes Victor's shoulder gently, and tries to comfort him by explaining the
situation.

ITARD: Victor, I cannot take you for a walk. . . .
I am ill. . . . I'm going to see the doctor. . . .
Ill! Do you understand? So you stay here.

He takes the hat from Victor's head, puts it on his own,
and goes out. Immense disappointment appears on Victor's face. He goes up to his room.

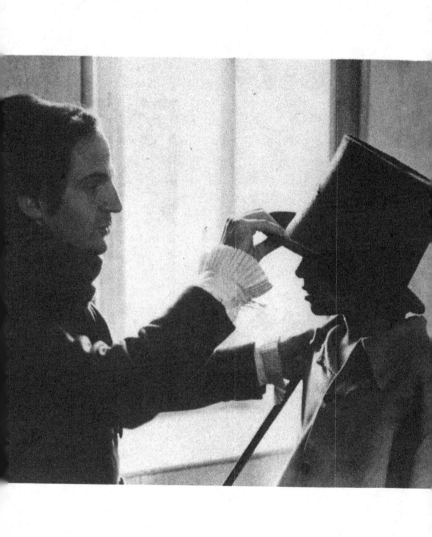

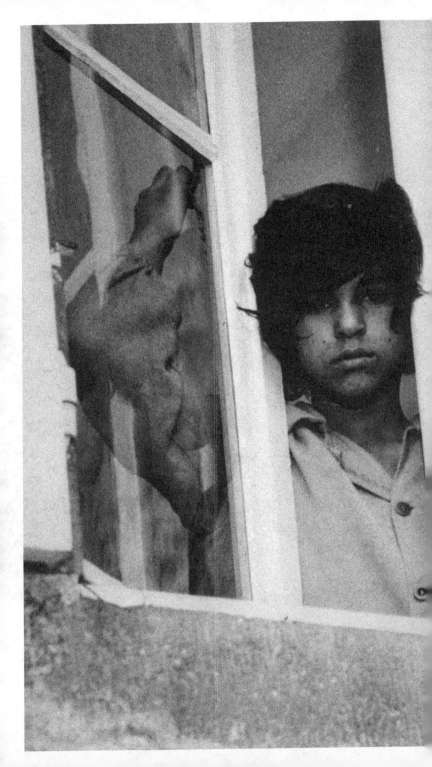

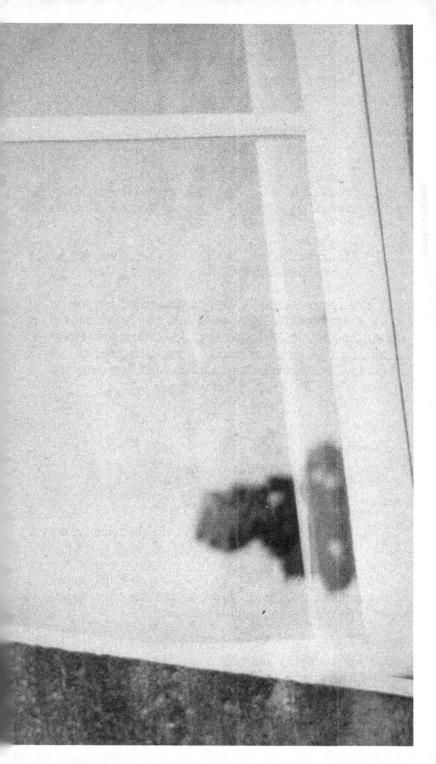

Itard's house.

Interior day.

The kitchen is empty. We can hear Madame Guérin's voice:

> MADAME GUÉRIN (*V. O.*): Victor, dear, go get me some water.

Victor comes toward us, carrying a pitcher. He goes to the water reservoir, is about to turn the faucet on, but he stops and looks toward the door, then toward the window. He puts the pitcher down and goes to the window, strides over, looks back inside a last time, and runs away.

Countryside.

Exterior day.

Victor is running across a field in the direction of the forest.

Woods: In the woods, Victor strides over the stones along the brook, bends down toward the clear water, and drinks as before, lapping the water.

In the deep forest: Victor tries to climb a tree, but he has lost his agility and falls down. He lies down in the dead leaves, exhausted.

Later. Victor has fallen asleep.

Itard's house. Office.

Interior night.

Itard is worried. He's pacing up and down in his office. He goes to the window.

Forest. Night: Victor is asleep in his bed of dead leaves.

Itard's office: Itard is sitting on his bed wearing a dressing gown. The clock strikes.

Forest. Dawn: Victor comes out of a thicket, picks up an acorn from under an oak, tries to eat it, then throws it away, disgusted. He goes on walking, taking a path to a farm. We hear dogs barking and chickens cackling.

Victor ventures into the farmyard which is still asleep. A dog on a rope barks at him. Victor goes into the chicken coop at the very moment when the farmer's wife opens a window on the second floor. She yells at Victor, who dashes out of the chicken coop with a chicken under his arm.

> FARMER'S WIFE (*yelling*): My chicken! . . . My chicken!

The farmer rushes toward Victor and makes him fall. In doing so, Victor lets the chicken go, then picks himself up swiftly and flees.

> FARMER: Thief! . . . Thief!

Victor runs rapidly down the road, followed by three peasants armed with pitchforks and sticks.

> PEASANTS: Thief! . . . Thief!

Country road. Day: Victor is running toward us. Suddenly he hears a carriage coming up behind him. Victor hides in the bushes along the road. The noise grows louder. We stay on Victor hidden, watching the carriage pass by.

Itard's house. Kitchen.

Interior day.

It is dawn. Itard is standing, his face worried; he pours himself a bowl of coffee. Madame Guérin, seated, is peeling potatoes. Itard puts the coffee pot on the table and goes to the window. He looks outside.

> COMMENTARY (*V. O.*): *I believe we shall see Victor no more.*

Itard's office.

Interior day.

Itard, wearing a frock coat, is at his stand, writing.

> COMMENTARY (*V. O.*): *I can affirm to Your Excellency that he had attained the free use of all his senses: he furnished constant proof of attention, recognition and memory. He could compare, discern, and judge; in a word, apply all the faculties of his understanding to objects relating to his instruction. This child of the forest had managed to endure the confinement*

of our quarters, and all these happy changes had come about in the short space of nine months.

Dining room.

Interior day.

Close-up of the letter addressed to: "His Excellency, Ministry of the Interior."

> COMMENTARY (*V. O.*): *I must thank Your Excellency for your trust. . . . Unfortunately, young Victor has escaped.*

We see Itard in a three-quarter shot from the back, sitting at his desk. Through the window Victor appears, crestfallen and exhausted. He looks inside the room. Seeing a shadow pass across his paper, Itard turns around all of a sudden. He sees Victor, and dashes to the French doors.

> ITARD: Victor! . . . Victor!

Shot of the window: In the garden Itard appears, running after the child.

> ITARD: Victor!

Victor, frightened, wants to escape, but Itard catches him and tenderly leads him back into the house.

> ITARD (*calling*): Madame Guérin! . . . Madame Guérin! . . . Look . . . Victor's back!

Madame Guérin enters and hugs Victor.

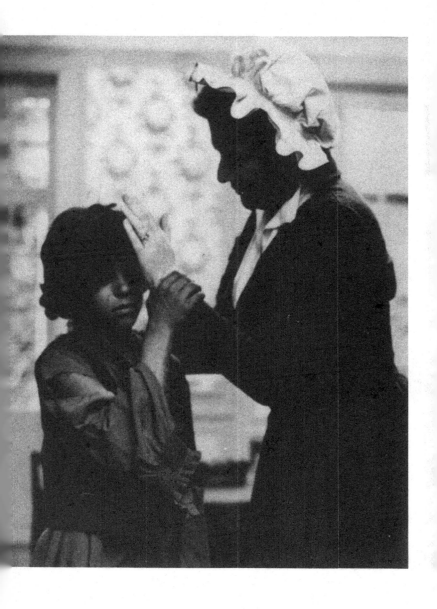

MADAME GUÉRIN (*happy and astonished*): Who brought him back?

ITARD: Nobody. He came back by himself.

Madame Guérin kneels down in front of Victor. She is deeply moved.

MADAME GUÉRIN: That's my boy. My boy has come home all by himself. You're in tatters, but you're here.

Victor takes Madame Guérin's hand and rubs it against his face. She lets him do it, then gets up to kiss him on his forehead. Finally, she pushes him toward Itard, who takes the child by the shoulders.

ITARD: I am glad, Victor. You have come back home. Do you understand? . . . You're at home. (*He strokes his hair.*) You're no longer a savage, even if you're not yet a man. (*Itard pauses for a while, trying to hide his emotion.*) Victor, you're an extraordinary youth, a youth of great promise. (*To Madame Guérin*) Madame Guérin, take him up to rest.

Madame Guérin and Victor go up the stairs as Itard watches them.

ITARD (*very calm*): This afternoon, we shall resume our lessons.

Madame Guérin and Victor are climbing the steps. Victor turns around to look at Itard. *Iris out* on Victor's face.

Printed in the United States
By Bookmasters